INNOCENT

INNOCENT

Amy Kulp

First paperback edition May 2022.
First ebook edition June 2022.

ISBN 9798985930900 (paperback)

Published by Amy Kulp

For business inquiries, contact amy.kulp1@gmail.com
For more information, visit the author's webpage at
http://amykulp.weebly.com

To my mom. Without her love and support, I would have never believed in myself.

Chapter One

"Don't. Touch. Me." I gritted my teeth and yanked my shoulder away from the hand that was planted on it. I forced myself up and hurriedly opened up the door. Since it was after school, I knew that I wasn't being followed. Everyone who stayed was probably practicing for whatever sport, program, or club they were a part of. When I checked the hallway in case of stragglers and didn't find any, I ran to the nearest bathroom stall and cried.

***

"You need to bring that energy more." I smiled but kept punching the bag as hard as I could. My trainer, Missy, rarely gave out compliments like that. She steadied the bag for me and I hit harder as her compliment radiated throughout my body. "Stance." I was forced to look at my posture and change my position. After all of this training, I still couldn't manage to fix my form without her telling me that I needed to. "Alright, I think that's good for today." She moved from the bag and looked down at the bandages around my knuckles. They were starting to be speckled with light red droplets. I couldn't help but smile at accomplishing this. It meant I worked extra hard. "Let's go practice in the ring."

I nodded and grabbed my water bottle. Nothing like working up a sweat and then tasting that first drink of ice water. It almost always sent a painful tinge down my throat until I could get used to it. I barely got any in my mouth though. I hung it over my face in desperation to cool my body down. When the water overflowed from my mouth and dribbled down my chin and onto my bra, I couldn't help but stare at my abs. Mixed with the water and my sweat, they were glistening under the overhead lights.

"Tanner!"

I blushed red as I realized that I was just caught enticed with my own body. Not wanting to make Missy mad, I ran over to the benches. I prepared myself by removing my shoes and massaging them for a few seconds to help soothe their aches. She did not like shoes in the boxing ring because of the scuffing they made. When my feet were done with their preparation, I took notice of my hands. I had to apply new bandages since blood was visible. Another gym rule. Once my new bandages were on, I took my hair out of the sagging ponytail and repositioned it higher off of my neck. I hated when my hair touched my skin. The last essential tool I needed from my bag was my mouthguard. While it wasn't required to have one in, I was not taking my chances with Missy. She was a powerhouse and could knock my teeth out. I didn't want to have any missing teeth since the school year was starting soon. I needed to make a good first impression.

"You ready?" she asked as I stepped into the practice ring with her. I nodded my head before she glanced over at the headgear that I had forgotten about. If it's not in my bag, I usually forget about it. I growled in response when I placed a spare on and she smiled at me. She put her mitts up and I struck them. Right, left, right-left-left, kick. "I need you madder!" she yelled. I growled at her and hit harder. "You're being predictable! Catch me off guard!" I pounded harder and harder until I felt the blisters begin to reopen. "Come on, Tanner!" I hit again and kicked. Losing my balance, I felt myself fall on my back. When I opened my eyes, Missy was smirking down at me. "I think we're good for today."

I needed to work on my balance. She threw the mitts off and helped me up. She instantly hit my head playfully and I knew she wasn't mad. I did not want to disappoint her by forgetting the simple forms I should be practicing. When I got down near the bench, I took the headgear off and popped my mouth guard out. When I finished placing everything back in my bag, I tried to relax on the bench.

"Is the AC even on?" I yelled.

"It's on high Tanner," she replied. "Quit complaining. You don't hear Aaron moaning."

I hated when she compared me to other people. I was my own person. It pissed me off even more that the comparison was with Aaron. While there was nothing wrong with him, she only compared us because we were similar in age. Everybody else was either a child or an adult. Besides, from what I had gathered about Aaron was that he was only allowed to train here because he worked here. Missy had a scholarship program where people can train discounted or free depending on how much they wanted to work. Rumors I had heard through the grapevine are that she gave Aaron an even bigger discount than most people because he was bullied at school. I have never seen him train, but if he was so great, why couldn't he defend himself?

Realizing that my body was not going to cool down on its own, I grabbed my bag and headed towards the showers. Since boxing was a male-dominated sport, I usually had the locker rooms to myself. I always kept my bag on me, but if I wanted to, I could keep my bag in here without worrying about anything being taken. So when I saw that the coast was clear, I stripped and found myself an empty stall. The cold water felt amazing on my body and I watched as it washed the blood off of my skin. The open blisters were nasty to look at but it was something I thought was satisfying to see as well. No pain, no gain.

Finishing up, I shivered and wrapped a towel tightly around my body. I came back to my bag and dug out the clean clothes. The first thing I noticed about it was the soft scent of fresh linen. I loved that smell but it wouldn't last long if it was near my bag. I needed to throw it in the wash too - it stunk.

Once I tied my sneakers and finger-combed my hair, I threw it up in a sloppy bun and headed towards the gym entrance. I patiently waited in the parking lot as I looked for my mom's car but it didn't arrive for another five minutes. I was surprised since she was usually early. I grinned as I approached the car to let her know that training had gone well but as I approached, it vanished when I saw who the actual driver was.

"Mom's running late from work so she told me to come and get you," my brother, Luke said. He rolled down the window to talk to me but I already had the backseat open to hear him. I placed my bag on the seat and felt like my voice was going to tremble as I spoke.

"I-I think I-I'll walk." I couldn't meet his gaze as I said this and he groaned in response.

"You're crazy." He rolled his window down farther and leaned over. "It looks like it's going to rain and this is a bad part of town."

"S-so?"

"You're only wearing a sports bra." I shrugged my shoulders and looked up at the sky to see if he was telling the truth. "You're my little sister, if anything happens to you it would be my fault." I remained still as he tried talking me out of it. He must've known that I was stubborn and wouldn't change my mind though because he clasped his hand over my wrist. My first reaction was to flinch out of his grip.

"D-don't touch m-me."

"Chloe, are you okay?" I still refused to look at him, but I was able to hear Luke get out of the car. He stood taller than me by one inch, but it felt like he towered over me by one foot. My body shrank and I started shivering even though my body was still sweating.

"D-don't call me C-Chloe!" I managed to yell. "It's T-Tanner."

"*Clo-ee.*" He smirked down at me and I felt tears overflowing from my eyes. I hated being called that. I finally met Luke's gaze and the smirk he had on before, had now vanished. I hated crying in front of people so instead, I decided to run.

I heard him yelling after me but I couldn't keep the tears from coming. I hated crying. I felt so vulnerable whenever I let my emotions out. That was one of the reasons I was taking boxing, so I could get all of my tears and anger out. Also so I could protect myself.

I ran down the street as if my life depended on it. I knew that people were staring at me like I was crazy, but it helped to ease my mind. As I continued to run, though, I knew that it would take me a while to get home. It took about ten minutes in the car and since I was not as fast with my running, it would probably take thirty or forty minutes. If anything, this could give me time to think. I heard that running was also a stress reliever. While I have never tried to do it besides cardio warmups, I could try to use it like that.

I had so many worries I could think about: new school, new friends, new teachers, reputation, not knowing the school layout, where I would sit during lunch, what clique I wanted to belong to. I was mostly worried about my reputation and who my new friends would be. I'm used to moving, which I tend to do every year. What if people had heard about me? Or what if they started looking me up online? I've looked myself up before and I haven't found anything juicy but that doesn't mean other people can't. This can deter people from wanting to be my friend. I usually am only able to make a couple of decent friends. Usually, once I move I don't keep in contact with them. Luke is the complete opposite though. He is always part of the popular group and makes friends easily. I'm always jealous of him.

When I got home, I was the first one back. No cars were in the driveway which meant my mom, dad, nor Luke had made it yet. My dad was probably still at work. I haven't figured out his new hours yet to know for certain though. My mom worked around the clock and was constantly having important meetings. It felt like she valued her work more than her family sometimes. I know she tried though. I think that Luke was still looking for me, but I wouldn't be surprised if he stopped for fast food instead.

I knew that we had a spare key under one of our loose stepping stones so I grabbed it out of place. I was still nervous that Luke was going to arrive and see me coming home, so my hands were jittery. I was barely able to put the key in, but once I was able to, I slammed the door shut and bolted to my room.

I could finally try to calm down now.

With my door now locked, I felt free enough to open my window. When I looked out, I noted how dark it was. Was it this dark when I got home? How was I able to see while running? If Luke was still looking for me, he wouldn't be able to tell if someone was me or just some random person running on the sidewalks.

When I grew bored with that, I turned my desk lamp on and pulled out my diary from the drawer. I often forgot to jot down my thoughts in this but I figured when I did remember it was good enough. I felt my nerves starting to calm down but when I thought about what I wanted to write on this page, I began to cry. Today's entry was barely two lines but they were starting to blur from the small teardrops covering them.

When I heard a car door slam shut, I pushed my diary back into my drawer. Even though my door was locked, I didn't want anyone to see me writing in it. It was embarrassing. What if they wanted to read it? When I knew my diary was secure, I flung my body to my bed. I pulled the blankets over me and pretended to be sleeping. If it was my mom, she would try to talk to me for hours. If I was asleep, she would get the hint and stop. If I was awake, she would somehow know. I had to make it look like I was sleeping for them to leave me alone.

"Are you in there, Chl... Tanner?" I heard Luke say. I felt my muscles tense as his voice grew louder at my door. "I don't know why you hate the name, Chloe. It's a beautiful name, that's why mom picked it. Anyway, I hope you're alright and nothing happened. Mom has pizza downstairs if you're wondering and your gym bag is by your door." I listened to some shuffling outside of my door and didn't let my muscles un-tense yet. "I'm sorry about earlier."

I was able to see light shining from underneath my door. I watched as the shadow moved away and the hall lights were then turned off. As I thought about what he said, my stomach growled. I forced myself to ignore it. I didn't want to see my family and while the food was alluring, I didn't want to talk about why I'm acting the way I'm acting. I always explain to them that I'm a teenager and I'm probably going through puberty, but none of them believe me. The fewer interactions I have with them, the better. Even if that meant I had to fake sleep until I actually fell asleep.

Even if that meant that I fell into a series of nightmares that I couldn't shake.

Chapter Two

"Chloe, can I talk to you after class?" my science teacher asked as he pulled me off to the side. I nodded yes but hoped it wouldn't take too long. No matter how much I rushed and ran to get to my next class, I was always late. It was in the farthest corner of the school too. I tried talking to the other teacher about why I'm always late, but they didn't care. I tried every solution I could think of - having my books with me before the class, not talking to friends in the hallways, and briskly walking from class. Nothing worked! How was I supposed to make it within two minutes? It wasn't like it was an important class either. It was study hall. The teacher was crazed over study hall. "I'll give you a hall pass."

I nodded my head with more distinction this time. While I was glad that I would not have to worry about being tardy again, I was worried about what he wanted to talk about. My grades were not the best, but I wasn't failing. I also wasn't worried about my attendance in class since I was always on time. I don't remember being disruptive to where I would have to be warned either. It was poor timing on his part because, for the rest of his class, all I could think about was what he could want to talk about. I ran through about one-hundred scenarios in my head before I heard the bell ring.

I didn't want anyone to know that the teacher needed to speak to me so when they started filing out, I packed up slowly. I pretended that I would be leaving with everyone else, but when the room was empty, I stopped the charade. I saw some students looking at me as if they knew that I would be getting in trouble, but I knew that I was just being paranoid. Some people darted their eyes from me to the door while others kept eye contact with me. Did they know something I didn't?

I didn't have a lot of friends at this school. I had a couple but none of them were in this class. The friends I did have, weren't good enough for me to ask them about the gossip. I wasn't really that type of girl to want to know. That was something for the popular clique - I wasn't a part of that group. If I had to classify myself, I would say I'm nerdier than I would admit out loud. Luke was the popular one out of both of us. Every school we went to he was able to always make friends. It helped that he was better looking now that he was done with puberty. I was still going through it so while Luke had clear skin, I had acne, while Luke had a better smell, I had to repeatedly put deodorant on throughout the day, while Luke could workout without a sweat, I found that I could only wear certain colors. I wish I could have the confidence that he had every time we went to a new school. That confidence was key. He could go into a group of strangers for five minutes and all of them would want to get to know him better - he was natural at that. I would feel like I was forcing myself. It was getting to the *point where I didn't even want to make friends anymore. I had in-school friends but nobody I wanted to talk to outside of it. I would just leave them at the end of the year.*

My mom and dad were the reason we traveled. Specifically, their jobs. My mom is a successful businesswoman and my dad is an electrician. It wasn't very hard for him to find a job as electricians were needed wherever we went. I'm not exactly sure what my mom does though. It's enough to keep us wealthy and be able to move each year. Luke and I were both asked at one point if we would like to stay in one location but at the time we didn't. We wanted to travel the world. That was when we were younger though. Neither of us had any friends. I assumed in the years after our parents would keep asking us but they haven't. I also assumed when they saw that I had made friends and I enjoyed my last school, they would take the hint that I didn't want to leave them. They didn't though. We packed up and moved away. I don't see them anymore and I only text my one friend every so often. It's like I left them all behind.

How did Luke do it every year?

With our last school, I did have a boyfriend. I could brag about that since Luke has never had a girlfriend, just flings. My mom and my dad both were fond of my boyfriend as well. Luke approved of him too, but his approval didn't matter to me. Life was going fine and then one day... a tragedy happened. My mom and dad packed up and moved us away. Like usual. Unlike how it usually is, I didn't have time to mourn. I didn't have the resources or the familiarity to get all of my emotions out. I was left to figure it out myself. I felt like I ran away.

While I still was fond of my memories of my old life, it did help to be removed from the situation. The only real artifact I had of our relationship was a necklace he had given me. It was a small, silver heart with the letters T & C carved into it. Tanner & Chloe.

"Chloe?" I heard my teacher ask. Oh shoot, did he ask me something? I looked up to where I thought he was and was surprised to see he had moved. He was standing in front of me now. "Are you okay?" I nodded my head and pushed my glasses up my nose. I probably should have been focusing on what he wanted to talk to me about. The faster we were done talking, the faster I could worry about how my study hall teacher would react. "Well, like I was saying, I know you like extra credit so I was wondering if you would like to come after class and help me grade some tests."

"Why me?"

"The last test I graded was lower than usual. I don't want to see one bad grade affect your entire GPA." I felt my heart stop as he continued talking. "But if you come after-school once a week, I won't have to talk to your parents about it." Without thinking it through, I nodded my head. I needed a chance to fix my grades and if my parents didn't find out, that was even better. I could avoid the scolding and the low marks on my report cards. As we finished up solidifying the schedule, he wrote me a pass. I thanked him for the opportunity when he handed it *to me and turned to leave. "Oh and Chloe? We don't want to tell anyone about this opportunity." I crinkled my eyebrows in confusion. "It would be unfair for me to offer extra credit to one student without offering it to everyone."*

I nodded my head in agreement. It would be unfair to other students to know about this opportunity. It was unfair in general but I wasn't going to give up the extra credit. It benefited me! I promised him that I wouldn't tell anyone.

I kept that promise.

***

I woke up in pitch darkness and I could tell that I had been panting in my sleep. My breathing was staggered and my chest hurt from the constant in and out movement. When I calmed my breathing down and my body was no longer shaking, I turned my bedside lamp on. I clutched the chain that was dangling from my neck and tried to look at the engraving on it. Somehow this item was always able to calm me down. It was the only item that had sentimental value to me. My body was warm from the blankets, but the pendant was cool in my hand. The contrast gave me goosebumps along my skin. When the pendant was finally warming up, I sat up in my bed and flipped it over in my hands. I was slowly waking up but wanted to fall back asleep. As I felt my mind begin to relax, I felt my body growing weaker. I took the necklace off and threw it across the room. While I loved the original meaning behind the necklace, the nightmares I had from it outweighed them. I laid my body back down and maybe it was the sleep deprivation but I didn't care where it landed. I was too tired.

And I fell back asleep within seconds.

***

"That's a beautiful necklace."

"Oh, thanks," I said timidly. "My boyfriend... ex-boyfriend gave it to me." I clutched the necklace and pressed the pendant against my skin for comfort. Every time someone mentioned it, I grew self-conscious about it. Mostly because I was embarrassed to admit that he was no longer my boyfriend. Correcting myself every time someone mentioned it, made it seem like I was a crazy ex-girlfriend who couldn't get the boy out of her head. It made me sound delusional. I didn't like talking about him though. It felt like a fresh bruise that I kept poking to figure out where it came from.

"Can I see it?"

"Sure, let me just take it off, fir..." I straightened my back when he grabbed it from my hands. His movements felt forced and planned. He didn't let me finish my sentence before deciding he was going to take charge to touch it. He stared at the pendant intently and it made me uncomfortable to have him so close to my body. "I think I should take it off, then you could look." I reached

around my neck and undid the hook. When I took it from around my neck, I showed him it and he put it in his hands. He kept flipping it over and over again and I wasn't sure what he was exactly doing. There wasn't that much to look at. It was silver and had T&C engraved in it.

"He must've been something special." I nodded my head and reached for the necklace back. My neck felt naked without it. As if he knew it was my next movement to grab for it, he immediately moved his hands out of my reach and continued to look at it. "Is it of sentimental value?"

"Um… yeah."

"Tell your boyfriend that he's lucky."

"Uh, thanks?" I questioned. I was beginning to get a bit uncomfortable. What could that possibly mean? It felt wrong for him to say those words in that exact order to me. "But, he's an ex…"

"Oh, I'm sorry."

"Me too." I reached for my necklace but he still didn't give it to me. "Can I, please, have my necklace back?"

"Sure." I reached my hand out but he didn't give it to me. Instead, he walked behind me and pushed my hair away from my neck. I felt the goosebumps on my neck prickle as his warm hands came close. He wrapped the necklace against my neck and took his time hooking it up. As soon as he was done, I shot out of my seat and ran for the door. That wasn't normal and I knew that it wasn't normal. He was too close.

I was uneasy about it and knew that what he was doing was weird. While I have had people help me put this necklace on, it didn't take as long as he did. It felt like he just wanted to be near me and that putting that necklace on was the way to do that. From that point forward I knew that I wasn't going to take it off around him. He had seen it once and that is all he needed to remember it. I also felt careless enough to let him hold it. What if he would've broken it?

I promised myself that I wouldn't take it off for anyone. I had kept that promise to myself for an entire year.

***

When I woke up, I knew that I was going to be sore before I tried to move. I felt a slight burn in my knees and my lower back. I woke up hunched over my legs that were crossed on top of each other. Considering that I wasn't very flexible, I was impressed that it didn't hurt worse than it did. I knew how to alleviate my joints though and slowly started rolling my ankles and wrists. I worked my way up to the elbows and knees until I started relaxing and rolling my entire body. Even when I laid back down, my back cracked. While satisfying to hear and feel, I would have been grossed out thinking about someone else cracking like that. I would probably be a little worried too. When I looked to the side, I saw the time and groaned to myself. I have never slept past nine.

Here I was still stuck in bed at ten. I slowly tried getting out of bed again and heard my legs crack from their stiffness. I don't know how I had fallen asleep in that position, but I hoisted myself up again and listened to an echo of cracking.

Being that it was ten in the morning and that it was also Monday, I assumed nobody was home. My mom would be at work. My dad would be at work. Luke never stuck around the house and was constantly hanging out with people. Even though we haven't had the first day of school yet, I was confident that he made some sort of friends already. He was a natural at it.

I changed from my old clothes to some new ones without a glance at what they looked like. I needed to go to the gym and nobody judged me on what you were wearing. I hated feeling my hair on my neck, so I pinned it into a messy twist and yawned. I couldn't remember anything from last night so it was either a really good dream or a terrible nightmare. Since I was yawning and still exhausted, that had to mean it was a nightmare. When I finally forced myself to look in the mirror, I took a great inspection of my face and saw that the bags under my eyes were swollen and that I had crust in my eyelashes. I was too lazy to pick it out so I let it go. I knew that it would bother me later. Not remembering what I dreamt about and the crust in my eyelashes indicated to me that I had also been crying last night. Whatever it was that had made me cry, must've been terrible. I guess there was a plus side to not remembering your dreams. Even without remembering, I knew there were only about two things that would make me cry. Even thinking about it made me cringe.

When would this torture stop?

Without thinking about yesterday's incident, I unlocked my door and immediately kicked my bag. Thankfully, nothing strong or heavy was in there or I may have hurt my toe or the item. Out of annoyance, I threw the bag back into my room and continued to walk down the hallway and steps. It was too early to think rationally about anything.

I grabbed a cereal box off of the top of the fridge and poured milk directly into the box. I started scooping it out with a spoon and smiled to myself. Cereal was the one thing that I could eat all of the time. There were so many different brands and flavors that I could never get bored.

"Honey, are you okay?"

I jumped with the box still in my hand. Nobody was supposed to be home. Why was someone home? I turned around to face my mom and planted a guilty smile on my face. There was no way my mom couldn't see me doing this. Maybe she wouldn't say anything about it though. I nodded my head and her lips formed a thin, straight line. Why was she home? She is always at work at this time. My mom has never been late. She always has to be somewhere fifteen minutes early. I think it's an anxious thing but she has instilled that mantra into my head as well. I needed to be fifteen minutes early for everything as well. I knew she didn't take a sick day because she was dressed in her normal business attire. Besides, my mom doesn't use her sick days or personal days. She loved to work and she was very driven to work. This is why I was so confused as to why she was still here.

"Luke told me what happened yesterday. What was that about?" I shrugged my shoulders and continued eating my cereal. She looked at me disapprovingly but didn't say what she was thinking. "You've been distant with him ever since we moved. Is everything okay?"

"I'm fine," I grumbled. Why did she have to have her motherly talk with me now? I was tired and it was clear that I had just woken up.

"He misses you, you know."

"I'm right here," I snarled back at her. If Luke missed me, he had a funny way of showing it. He rarely talked to me in the house and when he does have the opportunity to be with me, he complains the whole time. Even yesterday, he was complaining about having to pick me up. He apologized afterward but that was because he probably thought he would get in trouble. My mom's face saddened after I snapped at her though. Moms have a way of making you feel bad for anything you say to them and my mom was no exception. Instead of saying anything about it, she hugged me. When she let go, she seemed a bit startled and I couldn't help but be startled as well. "What?"

"Where's your necklace?"

I felt at my chest where the necklace usually was and felt panic-stricken when I couldn't find it. Instantly, I put the cereal box and spoon onto the table and immediately rushed upstairs. I had no idea where my necklace was. Maybe it fell off while I was sleeping last night? Maybe I didn't put it back on after I was done in the gym? I felt like I was hyperventilating just at the thought of possibly losing it.

When I got back into my room, I saw my bag on the floor where I had kicked it. Perfect opportunity to go through it. I undid all of the zippers and mildly flinched when the smell penetrated through the bag. I threw the worn pieces of clothing in my hampers and finally came down to sorting through the rest of it. A mouthguard, water bottle, earbuds, deodorant, hair ties, band-aids, drink packet, wrap. As I ended up picking the little crumbs out of the main compartment, I knew that neither the necklace nor pendant was in here. I tossed it aside and started searching through my room.

I tore the blankets, sheets, and pillows off of my bed and shook them out. Nothing banged to the ground and I started searching my floor for it. I needed to vacuum with how much hair was on there. I guess I never realized because I usually wear socks around the house to keep my toes warm. Even though I was repulsed by it, I continued searching. I inspected underneath my bed, under my chair and desk, under anything I could peek under, and under everything I could think of. I still could not find my necklace. It had to be lost. When I saw it near my closet, I took a moment to just breathe a sigh of relief.

I crawled over to it after a moment of controlling my breathing. I picked it up delicately but watched as the chain ran through the pendant. When the entire chain was picked up and the pendant didn't come along with it, I felt tears collecting in the corners of my eyes again. I broke my pendant. I couldn't just replace this. The chain wouldn't be the same and it wouldn't have come from the boy I loved. This was the only item I had to remind me of him. I wasn't even sure how it had gotten over here. Maybe from shaking everything out and turning my room upside down.

"Are you okay? Did you find it?" my mom asked. She came into my room and crouched down next to me. When she realized that I was holding it, she put her hand on my back and felt me sobbing. It felt like I had gotten approval to continue, so I let out audible cries now. "Honey, it's only a chain. Nothing to worry about, I could replace it." I'm sure she thought that was reassuring but to me, it wasn't. It felt like she was trying to replace a huge part of me with something new.

"Mom!" I wailed. I hiccuped when I tried to stop myself from crying. "I can't just replace it, that's like replacing him." I sniffled a bit and hiccuped again. She would never understand. My dad was her first and only love. She never had to suffer through a breakup. She never had to suffer through a death of a loved one either. Yes, she liked him and approved of him but she would not know what it was like to lose him. I never got a chance to grow older with him. I never got a chance to see if we would work in the real world. I was stolen of these opportunities.

"Chloe-"

"Mom, it's Tanner," I replied.

"Chloe Leanne Duff," mom said sternly. I picked my head up and let the tears fall down my cheek. "I named you Chloe for a reason."

"Please. Please call me Tanner? Everyone else agreed."

"Why?"

I pondered what to tell her. I obviously can't tell her the real reason why I hate the name, Chloe. This was the first time that someone had questioned me on why I wanted my name changed. After an entire year, someone had finally had the guts to ask me. Now that I was asked, I didn't know what to say. I had never prepared for this and I knew I couldn't tell her the truth. She was my mom. I couldn't worry her.

"Besides, Tanner's a boys' name."

"Mom, this necklace, his ringtone, and his name are the only things I have left with him. I can't even see his grave because we moved."

"We thought it would've been better."

"Then why didn't you ask me first?" I paused. "I left Tanner and Summer." My mom's eyes were crinkled. "Summer just lost Tanner and then she lost me. Thanks, Mom. You did everyone a favor." I knew that I was being rude to her and I knew that I was overreacting. I knew what I was saying was going to hurt her, but I didn't want to replace my chain. I have been replacing everything in my life. Every year. I was tired of change. I wanted my life to be constant. Didn't my mom ever want that?

My mom nodded her head and just left my room without saying another word. I knew that she would just brush off this conversation as me being a hormonal teenager. Maybe part of it was. She didn't understand that I had such a hard time feeling accepted every year. Tanner and Summer were my best friends who had made me feel included. It was the first time I had felt like I belonged somewhere. I just didn't understand why she was so comfortable with throwing my memories of Tanner away. The only person I knew that knew the amount of pain I was in, was Summer. I picked up my phone and immediately dialed her.

"Hello?" I listened to her groggily speak nonsense for a few minutes before I realized that there was probably a small time difference. "Chloe, what do you want?" I cringed when she said my name. "It's like... four in the morning."

"I need someone to talk to."

"Talk to your mother," Summer replied.

"We fought."

"Really?" I cringed when I heard her voice become happy. She loved listening to other people's drama. I'll admit that I do too but I try to seem as disinterested as I could. "I mean... Really?" I smiled again when she attempted her sad voice. "What was it about?"

"Tanner..." I waited to hear some sniffling or movement but she stayed perfectly still and perfectly quiet on the other end. She wouldn't understand since I haven't called her since my move. I guess now was a good time to catch her up. "I keep having everyone call me Tanner-"

"Why? That's just torturing yourself, Chloe."

"I... I can't tell you."

"Then why did you call? We haven't called each other since Tanner died. I told you to ring me whenever you could and I sat and waited patiently. Eventually, I grew tired of waiting and I started living my life." Summer paused for a moment, probably biting her lip. "Chloe, I will never call you Tanner."

"Please."

"Not only is that torturing me, but it's torturing you. Plus, Luke, your mom, and your dad. They were close with him too, remember? After all, they had to get close to their daughter's boyfriend."

"I have a really good reason." I paused and bit my lip again.

"I'm waiting."

"I'm afraid to tell you."

"Goodbye, Clo-ee."

I felt tears threaten to spill out of my eyes and down my cheeks. I thought that Summer would've understood this more than anyone. We used to be so close together that we completed each other's sentences. I felt my lip quiver and sucked the top and bottom lip in. My chin was quivering worse than before. I hugged my knees and slid onto my back.

I felt like I just got rejected from Summer. She was one of my best friends two years ago. While we didn't talk that much, I assumed that we could talk and catch up and it'd be like old times. That was not the case though. She seemed more distant and judgmental about what I was doing with my life. I wanted her to cry with me. I wanted to break down just once. I wanted her to break down with me. She should have understood.

I felt myself let go and I couldn't control the tears. At least I was crying in private this time. These past two days had felt like I was doing nothing but crying or sleeping. With the never ending nightmares, I was always exhausted when I woke up. While I wanted to sleep in, my mind wouldn't let me without having to suffer. At least if I was awake, I could control it. If I thought about anything bad, all I had to do was exercise and I'd feel better. It would take my mind off of everything.

I'm not sure what I was complaining about though. My parents both love me and so does my brother. I didn't have to worry about not eating or not having a place to sleep at night. While I felt like my parents didn't understand me, I never felt like they didn't love me. I knew that I couldn't just blame her and my dad for constantly moving either. We had all agreed on it. I couldn't keep blaming them for continuing to do what we all wanted. I wanted to blame her though. I wanted to be selfish. I wanted to blame them for not knowing, but I knew I had never told them I wanted to stay. Would that have even made a difference? Honestly, when I got into a relationship with Tanner, I thought that was enough of a clue that I didn't want to keep moving year after year. They never got the tip. Aren't parents supposed to read between the lines?

I let my hand go of the pendant and I listened to it clatter to the floor. In some ways, it made me a little happy and got worries off of my chest but it also gave me a big gaping hole in my heart. I was able to calm myself down to the point where I was just hiccupping or sobbing. When I was able to pick my head up off of the floor, I grabbed for the pendant again. It felt like I was hot and cold with this thing. As soon as I touched it, the familiarity of it made me smile. It should always be attached to me. I knew what I needed to do to calm down. I reached for my phone and listened to it ring. I wasn't expecting an answer.

"Hey, you reached Tanner's phone. If I'm not answering I'm probably out with my best friends Summer and Chloe! If it's my parents, I promise I'm not dead. Just leave me a message. No promise that I'll call back though."

"Hey Tanner," I felt myself say. "It's C... It's Chloe." I gulped. "I wish you were still here. I know that you would know exactly what was going on and attempt to help me. Of course, you probably would've prevented it from the beginning." I paused, not knowing what else to say. The silence on the other end was deafening and I knew that was the end of my call.

Before Tanner, I have never had someone close to me pass away. I didn't know how to react when I found out the news. I still don't know if I'm reacting normally or if I'm taking too long with the recovery process. While my thoughts about him and the phone calls to him have greatly decreased, I have found it soothing to call him. I was told journaling would help too but I often forget to do that. The necklace might seem like such a frivolous thing to be attached to but it makes me feel like Tanner is still with me. The entire necklace - not just the pendant and not just the chain.

I kept pressing the pendant into my hand until my knuckles were hurting and my nails were poking my hand uncomfortably. I probably laid on the ground for two hours total until my phone buzzed. I didn't bother checking it, I didn't want to talk to anyone at the moment. When it finally rang enough for it to go to voicemail, I sighed and turned my phone on to listen to it.

"Tanner!" I gulped. "I've heard that you weren't coming in today." I furrowed my eyebrows and realized that mom probably told her I wouldn't attend boxing today. "I'm just here to tell you to get off your sorry ass and stop pitying yourself." I began to chew the inside of my cheek. Missy was all about tough love and sometimes it worked. Other times, it didn't and just made me mad at her. "Plus, boxing is an amazing way to get out your frustrations." I heard some heavy breathing on the other end of the phone before she hung up. Knowing her, she was probably working out as she was making that call. I swear she never gave herself a day off.

I instantly knew that she was right though. Boxing was a great stress relief for me. It helped get rid of all of my anger and took my mind off of whatever it was that was bothering me. It was probably better to be surrounded by other people anyway. Whenever I was alone I made my situation ten times worse. Just constantly thinking about it over and over until I drove myself crazy. I knew that's what I was doing with the current situation too. That voicemail was enough for me though. I got up from the floor and looked at myself through the mirror. I cringed when I looked at my swollen eyes and the tear stains that ran down my cheeks. It was worse than when I had gotten up this morning and now they would be able to see what I was like before I had gotten her message. I quickly put my knotty hair in a ponytail and held my head when I felt the knots tug. I was too lazy to brush my hair.

Knowing that I didn't wash my gym clothes or equipment, I rummaged through the drawers in my room. I found some athletic clothes that would be acceptable for today but knew I needed to wash them when I got home. They were a little snug and a bit too small which is why they were sitting at the bottom of my drawers. Slightly too small clothes were better than stinky clothes though. I made sure to repack all of the equipment I would need before running down the stairs.

Running as softly as I could, I tried sneaking out before my mom could stop me. I wasn't sure if she was home but was hoping that she wasn't. I didn't hear the door slam shut for her to go to work though. As soon as I went down the stairs, she stopped me. When I looked over, she was now in pajama bottoms with a hot cup of tea. She was smiling and was glad to see that her plan to get me to stop crying was working. I smiled politely at her and she nodded at me.

I was forgiven for how I acted.

I grabbed a water bottle from where we kept it next to the doorway and bolted out. I had to do this before she wanted to talk to me. Although I had a couple of questions for her. Why was she at home? Did she quit her job? Was she sick? My mom rarely ever stayed home. Working is her main personality trait. While I loved that about her, I didn't get to see her a lot. Especially growing up, she would concentrate on work too much. Sometimes I just wanted her to be my mom and spend time with me. I knew there wasn't an easy balance and she was doing the best she could, but it was hard with her always working.

I decided that instead of walking to the gym, I was going to run. I probably should have stretched because of how sore I was from my sleep, but I was already on the move. I wish that I had timed my run from the gym to home yesterday because I wanted to set a personal best time. Breaking my personal bests was my favorite thing to do. It motivated me to be better every single day I did something. The only motivation for today's run was the dark clouds that were clouding the sky. I do not want to get caught in it if it starts to rain.

My wish was not granted. Within a few seconds, I felt a droplet hit my head. If it stayed like that, I could deal with it. As I ran through the rain and started seeing the puddles splashing more rain, I knew that it was going to get worse before it got better. I didn't even think to check outside to see if I would need a jacket or umbrella though. I continued to run as I felt my shirt clinging to me and grew self-conscious. These clothes were tight without the rain, but now that they were wet, they were sticking to my body like a bodycon dress. I needed to be prepared for these types of things. I would have to make a mental note to pack something in my bag for emergencies like these. I eventually had to stop running because I was unable to see two inches in front of me. I walked with my head down and my hands protectively covering my bag. While it sucked to be stuck walking in this, I couldn't imagine driving right now in this downpour. I wouldn't be able to see the road. Good thing I didn't ask my mom for a ride. I would've felt guilty if she drove in this. It is why I was surprised to see a car pull over and honk at me though.

Nothing about the car looked familiar to me.

I decided to just ignore them. It wasn't my dad's, mom's, or Luke's car. I didn't know that many people in town either so I wasn't sure who it could be. The only person I knew who wasn't related to me was Missy. I didn't know any of my neighbors because I wasn't interested in meeting them. I figured that I would make friends in school or boxing. However, I had kept mostly to myself. I was not focused on making friends, I was focused on protecting myself. I, unfortunately, did not know what Missy's car looked like. So if it was her, she would have to figure out a new way to get my attention.

"Tanner!"

I walked past the person who had shouted my name. I didn't acknowledge them and I didn't give them an indication that I heard them. They had to have known me though if they knew my name. Right? I looked back once and was surprised to see that he had pulled over and had gotten out of his car. In an instant reaction to having him right behind, I kicked him where it probably hurt. When I was able to see who it was, I gasped.

"Oh gosh, I'm sorry Aaron!" His body almost completely crumbled to the ground as he tried to process what had happened. "I didn't know it was you." He looked up at me with a grimace and I could only imagine the pain he was in. "To be fair, you shouldn't sneak up on a girl who knows boxing." I placed my hands firmly on my hips as if that was good enough reason for me to have hurt him. He shook his head as he started getting drenched and I felt bad for him again.

"It's raining," he squeaked. He placed his hand on my shoulder to steady himself and I instantly tensed. I hope he didn't notice that. "And I thought you might want a ride." He shrugged his shoulders and started easing off of me. As he did so, my body started relaxing again. I didn't sense any ill-intention from him, but I had to keep myself guarded against him. "I didn't know exactly who you were." I didn't say anything but felt my body becoming more relaxed now. He was no longer touching me. "That's what we do around this neighborhood."

"C-Can you w-walk?" I asked making sure to change the subject. He didn't respond, but he did look up at me. His eyes looked like slits and he was staring daggers at me. I knew that I should be more skeptical around Aaron, but he was the nicest person I have ever met. His threat level was down to the ground. "But seriously, I'll just walk."

"You can't!" He looked up at me and pointed to my lips. "The walk is far and your lips already look like they're turning blue." My hand immediately shot up to cover my lips at his comment. I didn't know if he was being serious or not. I didn't want to admit it, but I was starting to get cold. I didn't want to accept his offer though. I didn't know him that well. Although I did think he was super nice, was that a reason for me to trust him? "Besides, your shirt is soaked and you never know where creeps are." I had to admit that I laughed out loud for that one. I don't know why it was funny to me, but from his expression, he was purposely trying to get something out of me. "Just come on, it's a ride."

He tugged me over to his car and my body tensed again. It felt odd to have someone trying to help me. Normally, people left me alone if I left them alone. I am nice to everyone, but I don't go out of my way for everyone. Why was Aaron? I have never had someone who was trying so hard to help me. Even though I barely knew him, it felt like he cared about my wellbeing. He pulled open the door for me and ushered me inside before slamming the door and getting in on his side. Once in, I buckled my seatbelt and crossed my arms over my chest. Now that I was out of the rain, I knew that I was cold. Maybe Aaron was right about the blue lips. I shivered from lack of heat and he looked at me out of concern.

"Are you cold?" he asked. I nodded my head no so he wouldn't worry and he laughed at me. Despite my protest, he turned the heat on and faced it so that it was blowing towards me. I was able to position my body closest to the door and I let my body hold onto the handle. Just in case. "Are you okay?" he asked. I unintentionally flinched from his voice. "Tanner?" Him saying the name I wanted to be called made me feel better. Although I wasn't sure if he knew my actual name. Maybe he thought it was Tanner.

He didn't try talking to me after that and it helped. I kept looking at the time to try and predict when we would arrive. It was hard to see outside and as the rain picked up, I was glad that Aaron stopped. I had goosebumps going up and down my arms from the chill. The longer the ride took to get to the gym, I found myself getting more relaxed around him. His not bombarding me with a million questions helped. It was like my aura was feeding off of his aura. If he wasn't nervous, I wasn't nervous. If he were nervous, then I would be nervous. I looked over at him as he drove and admired him for a second. My cheeks blushed at the thought and I couldn't stop thinking about how much longer it would be until we got into the gym. My mind instantly switched so that I was preparing myself for all of the bad things that could happen. It wasn't that I didn't appreciate the ride from Aaron, it was that I was afraid of what he could do while we were riding together. Aaron and I both knew boxing but he was better at it than me. He trained here longer and he knew Missy longer. I also knew that he was taking these classes to help stop people from bullying him at school. He was capable if he wanted to.

Although I haven't yet been to this school, I could only assume the worst for me. I could not wrap my head around anybody hurting Aaron. His appearances did make him seem like a string bean, but as soon as he started boxing, I was afraid of him. I knew that he had this aura of respect around him by how he held himself at these practices. People respected him because of his talent and skill. He had worked to get that reputation. He did all of the heavy liftings. Nobody could take that away from him.

"Don't worry, you won't catch me," he hastily said. I focused my attention back on him and realized that it must've looked like I was staring at him. Did he think I was afraid to be seen with him? He should know by now that I don't care what anybody else thinks. I am not that type of person. With his angry tone, came my fear that he could hurt me. It was off and on constantly. It was so tiring to think like this. I wish I didn't have to.

Before he could fully park his car in a spot, I opened the door and flew out of there. His little outburst in the car had made me feel uncomfortable again. I didn't even think about grabbing my gym bag from his car. I felt frenzied and panicked to where I couldn't think. Missy said hello briefly to me, but I couldn't muster up the courage to say a response back. Instead, I locked myself away in a bathroom stall. My heart was pounding because of how nervous I was and I searched for the pendant around my neck. It would help calm me down.

When I'm nervous and don't have an item that distracts my mind, it can get intense. I felt like I was having memory loss of where I could have put my pendant. I checked the pockets of my sweatpants but was only found with space. My mind went to horrible places and possibilities before I was struck with the obvious. I had left it in my bag. That bag was in Aaron's car. I cursed under my breath for a second and felt the tears beginning to form. That pendant helped me relieve my stress. I constantly just moved the pendant around the chain and it soothed out any thoughts I had. Without it, I had to think of new ways to cheer myself up from crying. I didn't like to cry in public. I didn't like to cry at all. I needed to be tougher than that. So I thought of inspiring words to help me banish the tears that were collecting in the corners of my eyes.

Tanner would not want me to be crying.

Summer would not want me to be crying.

Luke would not want me to be crying.

Mom would not want me to be crying.

Dad would not want me to be crying.

Missy would not want me to be crying.

Maybe, even, Aaron would not want me to be crying.

In one full moment, I shook my worries off of my back and walked out with a fake smile on my face. Before I officially hit inside the gym, I gave myself a last-minute pep talk.

Tanner, Summer, mom, Luke, dad, Missy, Aaron.

As soon as I got into the gym, I looked around the room. I wanted to be farther away from people than usual. The least amount of people was at the warmup and cardio area so I immediately hit the treadmills. I just wanted to make myself as busy as possible and since I wasn't sure whether or not Aaron brought my bag in, they were a great cardio exercise. I started slowly to work off the cold from earlier. When I felt my legs getting used to the exercise, I increased the climb and increased the speed. I was so in the zone that I even ignored a person who came next to me. They exercised on the treadmill and I found it a little aggravating since the other treadmills were empty. Why are they next to me? Maybe they wanted to out-compete me? Even if they didn't, I took it as a challenge and cranked my treadmill higher than theirs.

They didn't crank theirs up.

I looked up at them and immediately tripped over my foot. I turned it off when I regained my balance and even though I wanted to laugh at myself, I walked away. I saw the smirk on their face too and knew that it was hard for them not to laugh at me as well. I cleansed my treadmill and when I was done, I headed over to the punching bags. I didn't have my tape or my handguards since they were in my bag. That was in Aaron's car. Instead of prepping for it, I just started punching the bag. It stung my knuckles and I felt the skin beginning to tear away, but I was very emotional right now. I just wanted a release. My knuckles slowly started to lose the feeling in them so I was able to get in my rhythm. Aaron had different plans though. He held the bag in place so I was barely able to move it.

"Tanner, can I talk to you?" He reached for me but I flinched back.

Instead, I led myself to a bench and felt my breathing deepen. I was exhausted from running and prepping the bags, but I was nervous around Aaron. He didn't scare me. Him being a male scared me. Aaron came over to me anyway and when he lifted the water bottle to his mouth, I quickly took it out of his hand. I was too thirsty and since I didn't know where my bag was, I figured I could take a swig of his. He gave me a face that showed he was displeased with me but he let me do it. I wasn't sure if it was because of sympathy or he was a pushover. I gave it back, but by the time he got to it, there wasn't any water in it.

"Where's m-my bag?" I whispered.

"I'll go get it but stay here."

I nodded my head as Aaron ran out of the gym. He handed the bag to me and I fished out a water bottle for myself. I handed one to Aaron as well and he happily accepted, but a small red blush grew across his cheeks.

"Oh no, you didn't have to do that."

I pretended not to hear him. Instead, I grabbed the tape out of my bag and began wrapping my hands up. I'm not sure if Aaron thought we were really good friends now or what, but he kept trying to talk to me. I tuned him out and focused on my prep. My knuckles were already bloody and skinned. I just hoped Missy wouldn't see. She would lecture me the rest of the time I was here on how to better prepare myself. I heard that lecture so many times that I could recite it. When Aaron finally got the hint that I was ignoring him, he stopped talking. Strangely enough, he didn't move away from me. He didn't say a word as I prepped. Once everything else was put away and I was ready, I put an earbud in my ear and turned the music on.

I smiled at the song choice.

Instantly I went to the punching bag and began with my rhythm training. I didn't even attempt to notice that Aaron was still staring at me from a distance. It stayed like that for an hour and he only stopped watching me when he and Missy started talking. I was guessing he had to stop training and had to work now.

When Missy came into view, I unplugged my headphones and listened to her.

"You could be a little nicer to Aaron," Missy replied. I rolled my eyes as I continued punching the bag.

"He was only trying to help you." She sounded like she was trying to nag me as a teacher would. Maybe like my mom would.

"So, what? He's a tattletale now?"

"Tanner, this isn't like you." I saw the worry appear in her face as her eyebrows creased. "What's going on?" I punched the bag and she immediately held it. I jabbed at it but watched as it absorbed into Missy. "Are there family issues? Bullying? Nervousness because summer break is almost over and you have to start at a new school?"

"I've moved before," I simply replied. Missy seemed fed up with my answer but I didn't care.

"Whatever, Tanner. Just remember that Aaron knows what you're going through."

"He doesn't know anything," I whispered. I watched as Missy stopped to process what she heard. I knew she was just trying to help, but I didn't want her help. She had to have realized that. "And it's nothing."

Knowing when to give up, Missy let go of the bag and left me. She didn't bother me for the rest of the lesson but I did notice that she and Aaron kept staring at me.

Like I was an alien.

AMY KULP

Chapter Three

"I love you." A smile spread on my face as his lips delicately touched my forehead. "Will you be my girlfriend?" I nodded my head yes and he pulled me into a hug. His arms wrapped tightly around me, but it didn't feel suffocating when he did it. "I could just imagine Summer's reaction when we tell her." I chuckled a little as I thought about what her reaction could be. It would probably be funny and sarcastic and she would probably complain about being the third wheel. While the thought was nice, I couldn't help but sniffle when my nose began running again. I needed to escape the situation I currently was in before I could imagine Summer's reactions. "Stop crying, they can't hurt you if I and Summer are there."

"That's the problem, you guys aren't always there." I snuck a peek at him and his cheeks were sucked in. He hated feeling like he couldn't help me. "We barely have any classes together." I sniffed. "Oh, Tanner, why am I always the misfit at school?" He always knew how to make me feel better even if I was overreacting. He never made me feel bad for it. He listened and tried to give me advice. When I didn't want it, he would over exaggerate and I would see how silly I was being. He knew how to help me whenever I wanted it.

"They're just jealous," he cooed enthusiastically. He combed his fingers through my hair as we sat on the

girls' bathroom floor. He didn't care if he was caught in here though. He came because I had asked him to. Today's argument and the fight were the worst it had ever been. "What even happened?" It meant so much to me that he came to cheer me up even though he didn't know what had happened. It felt like someone finally cared about me and my emotions. It made me feel human.

"I was a bitch." He flinched when I cursed. I knew he hated it but I couldn't help myself. Sometimes I just needed to get a curse word out. It let him know how upset and angry I was. "I wasn't really in the mood for any taunting about..." I froze. Did he know the reasons I was constantly teased? How do you tell someone that?

"That you hang out with me and Summer?"

"Basically," I whispered. Even though he was trying to act like it didn't bother him, I saw a twinge of hurt on his face. He quickly masked it with his caring attitude towards me. "And I replied very snobbily that just because she looks pretty on the outside—"

"She had plastic surgery done. Plus she's rich and she wears tons of makeup."

"Tan-ner let me finish!" I knew that he was just saying this to cheer me up. Being rich did not mean you were rude. Having plastic surgery did not make you a bad person. Wearing makeup did not make you a bad person. I wanted to drive my point home though so I managed to sit myself up straight and I crossed my legs and positioned my body so I was staring at him. "Doesn't make her pretty *on the inside. Then all hell broke loose and she... decked me."*

"Where?"

"You're an idiot," I simply replied. He smiled at me. "It's where the big fat bruise is."

"Nose?"

"I didn't feel like fighting back so I just... cried. I felt so weak and—"

"It's okay to cry, love." I felt my heart melt. "It just means you were too strong for too long."

"That is so cheesy, Tanner."

"We all need cheesy and cliché moments in our life." His eyes sparkled and his smile glistened when he said that. He was so innocent that he believed that. He leaned in close to me so our faces were almost touching and I thought he was leaning in for a kiss. I leaned in too, but he didn't move closer. My cheeks blushed so I pulled away. I could tell that he was lost in thought. "But if they ever touch you again, you could take boxing lessons." He shrugged his shoulders. "For self-defense."

"No thanks, I don't believe in violence."

***

I heard my teeth clank onto the spoon as I bit into my cereal trying to decide on what movie I should watch. I have been in an angry mood lately and I was hoping that I could calm myself down by relaxing with my favorite cereal and a chick flick. As I bit into another spoonful, I knew that I would not be able to hear the movie as I ate. I heard a groan from the other couch as I put on subtitles. I rolled my eyes at Luke since I wasn't sure if he was complaining about the movie I chose or the fact that he had to read outside of school. Either way, I wasn't going to change my mind.

"Seriously?" He got up and stomped towards the landing of the stairs. "Spoiler alert, it's exactly like every other movie you watch. The boy and girl get together in the end."

"I need to w-watch this Luke!" I whined. Whenever he was home, Luke was always in control of watching TV. I didn't particularly waste my time watching it downstairs since I could watch it in my room on my phone. However, I wanted the experience. Hiding in my room would only make me angrier and more emotional. At least when I was downstairs I could socialize with family members so I didn't have to be alone. "I need a cliche moment!"

"Are you crying?" he asked. I sipped the milk in the bowl and ignored his question. While holding the bowl up to my face, I carefully checked my cheeks to see that they were damp. When did I start crying? "Are you PMS-ing?" he asked, cringing. He wasn't used to me showing so much emotion. I have cried every day this week. I'm not sure if it's because of the lack of sleep, stress from starting at a new school, or because I was about to start my period, but something was messing up my hormones. Luke hesitated for a moment before

AMY KULP

walking back over to the couches. Instead of taking the opposite one, he sat down next to me. My body tensed from the sudden movement, but I found that I could force myself to relax if I needed to. He seemed concerned right now.

"I'm just going through an emotional time right now."

It was clear that he didn't know how to comfort me. He grabbed the bowl from my hands and set it down on the table, but that only distracted me for two seconds. His body language even looked like he was uncomfortable. He was trying though. I will give him brownie points for that. Luke didn't understand that I didn't need to be shown I was cared about through physical acts. I just needed him in the room when I needed to vent. He could just pretend to listen and that would soothe my mind. Unfortunately, he started patting my hair. His movements were robotic and were like a Kindergarten student was trying to pet their dog. Did he think this would help me? I knew his intentions though. It felt comforting to know that he was here for me. There weren't too many moments like this between us. I immediately broke down and let myself cry because I felt safe enough to do so.

"I'm not so great at this stuff, Chlo-Tanner." I didn't care that he wasn't. I did appreciate him correcting my name though. All of these small gestures were comforting to me. Whether he knew it or not, in the long run, this would benefit our relationship. I continued to sob as I watched the film. "Maybe I should get mom."

He attempted to slip away from me but I grabbed his shirt. "N-no." He sat back down and I stopped myself from crying anymore. Clearly, I showed too much emotion too fast. Maybe I would need to do a little at a time. Or maybe I needed to control myself. What has gotten with me? I was used to bottling everything up. I liked to brag that I was good with it and was mature for my age. "I just need my brother."

"Are you sure?"

"No." We watched the movie for a moment without interruption. The silence between us was deafening, but the background noise from the movie made it bearable. "I'm afraid."

"Of?"

"Starting school tomorrow."

"You'll do fine and I won't let anyone hurt you." Lie. "You always do fine." Lie. "You'll make tons of friends, you always do." Lie. "You just never let anyone in." Truth.

"I think I'm going to bed."

"But you didn't finish the movie. You always watch movies until the end. You even watch the credits," he complained. Usually, he was complaining because I did this. Now he's complaining that I'm not? I snuck a peek at him while I was going upstairs and caught a look of pity and worry on his face. Maybe he cared about me more than I thought he did. He usually would bribe me to turn the movie off.

I sighed when I got up the stairs. I felt very angry and sad all of the time. The only time I was happy was if I was being nostalgic. However, the feeling of nostalgia usually made me feel empty and sad afterward. It was like I could not win. As soon as I was alone, I was thinking about the bad stuff in my life. Or about my experiences in previous schools. Or what I wanted to happen in the future. I was just loathing myself and wanted to be pitied, I guess.

Once I landed on my bed, I think I fell asleep instantly because the next thing I heard was my alarm going off. Automatically, I hit the snooze button and attempted to fall back asleep. Even though I wanted to try, I knew it was hopeless. I tended to stay awake after the initial wake-up. It was annoying at times, but other times when other people may have fallen back asleep and been late to work, I would not have been.

I huffed silently and groaned as I got up off of my bed. First day of school. Before doing anything with my appearance, I forced myself to shower and wash my body. This also helped me wake up so I wasn't so groggy and rude in the morning. I couldn't imagine starting the year off wrong because I was tired. Nobody would want to be my friend if I accidentally snapped at them for talking to me. I wouldn't even want to be my friend at that point. When I was out and dried, I took a quick look in the mirror and stared at my reflection. Last year, I looked so different. This year, instead of thin black glasses, I had my contacts in and my dark-under circles were disappearing from my eyes. It seemed that people who wore glasses had bags and circles under their glasses. My curly brownish-blonde hair was put back in a loose ponytail with it being straight from the shower I just had. I didn't even brush my hair anymore because it was useless. My skin was the olive-colored tone of a pale girl wanting to get tanned. Only this was my usual appearance. If I had let my hair down, it would fall past my shoulders and right above my chest. No blemish or beauty mark was present on my body unless you looked at the underwire of my bra. Which no one ever would. Ever again.

As I finished in my room, I grabbed my gym outfit and packed it into my bookbag. I didn't have time to come home after school so I knew I had to carry it with me all day. Depending on the size of my locker, I might be able to stuff it in there until later. I quickly ran down the stairs and into the kitchen. Once in there, I spotted an apple in the basket and decided that would be my breakfast. Whenever I had school or if I went to the gym in the morning, it was too early for me to eat. I could try but felt very sick afterward because I ate it as soon as I woke up. I could try to take a couple of bites but knew it'd make me sick later. I was hoping my walk to school would help drive me hungry, but if not, I hoped it would stay good until lunch. I preferred having my apples in the fridge, but I wasn't sure if this school had a place for students to put their lunches. I know most public schools don't. Without talking to anyone, I rushed out of the door and into the darkness.

I could have accepted Luke's offer to ride to school with him, but I wanted to be my own person. I needed to separate myself from Luke. In past schools, all of my friends had a crush on him and would only hang out with me so they could get to know him better. I have learned that if people didn't know I was related to Luke, they would like me for me. Later on, if they found out, it wouldn't be that big of a deal because I knew they were originally friends with me. Maybe Luke won't be popular at this school. I shook my head at that thought because I knew that wasn't true. He was already making friends just from hanging out in the neighborhood. I wish I could do that.

I could have also ridden the bus to school. I haven't ridden one of them in three years. Would they know where to drop me off? Would I know which stop is mine? Besides, there were always kids on there that were super loud in the morning. I can't imagine how I would react if they were bothering me this early. I preferred the quietness and thought it would be best if I just walked.

The walk to school was not that far from my house. I was thankful for that since the gym was an even longer distance. I could use this time for whatever I wanted - me time, exercising, thoughtfulness, studying time, and homework time. For me time, I could just focus on my future and the goals that I had. This time would help with things that I wanted to accomplish. If I wanted to exercise, I can pace myself at a low jog or do exercises on my way to school. Although that would be great for building muscle and my endurance, it would probably make me sweaty. I'm not sure if I'd be exercising too much before school. Maybe after school if I didn't have the gym. For the thoughtfulness period, I could just think about whatever I wanted. I could think about what might happen, what I might want to happen, or just daydream on my walk to school. Sometimes I needed to take a break from constantly pushing myself. Although it was hard for me to admit when I needed a break, I knew when I was over-exerting myself. If I had a huge test coming up, I could use that quietness for studying. I would just need to remember to have flashcards made the day before so that I don't have to lug multiple papers out of my backpack. Imagine if it was windy! I could also use it for homework I didn't finish the night prior. I knew this was a far-fetched idea, but if I was desperate enough I would be able to do it. It would probably be sloppy and I might not be able to see where I was going, but I would get it done before I got to school.

Since this was the first time I was walking to school, I felt myself beginning to get anxious. It was dark out and although street lights were hanging over the sidewalk, there weren't enough for me to feel safe. There weren't any cars on the road nor were their lights on in people's houses. I was alone, but it didn't make me feel comfortable. I knew as I began traveling the route more by myself that I would get used to it and it wouldn't provide so many emotions to me, but right now, all I could think about was the noise I was currently hearing. Or the bad things that could happen in the dark.

I immediately reached down to touch the pendant on my necklace before hitting my bare skin. My body froze in place and I tried touching the chain that should be around my neck. It wasn't there. When would I remember that I broke the necklace? I dropped my book bag on the pavement and looked through the belongings in there. I had to pack it in here, right? I know Aaron gave me my gym bag back so it should have been in the new bag. When I stopped searching, I huffed. I had a dilemma.

Did I want to go on the first day of school without my necklace? The first day of school is probably the most traumatizing and anxiety-inducing day. Today was the day that I would figure out which people could be my friends. It also was the day that I would find out which clique I would be a part of. I would probably be nervous in all of my classes because I wouldn't know anyone. I don't know what I would do without my necklace. What would my reaction be if I was angry? What if I was sad? Scared?

However, if I went back to my house, I would most certainly be late for school. It wasn't that I had already walked far, but walking back, finding the necklace, and then leaving the house again would cause so much time wasted. My parents would probably be up and they would want to talk for a couple of minutes before I went back out. I didn't want to ask my mom for a ride because I knew she planned her day out by the minute. I didn't want to ask my dad for a ride either because he didn't have to be at work for another hour. If Luke was there, I would ask him for a ride. However, I knew that he liked to arrive early on the first day of school. He did every year. After the first day, he would arrive just before the bell rang. The last resort would be the bus, but I'm not sure what time the bus would arrive to pick me up.

I chose to go back to grab my necklace. I wrapped my bookbag around me and held onto the straps tightly. It felt weird to run with it, but I needed to arrive on time so that I would make a good first impression on my teachers. Every time my legs fell behind me, they would kick the bag because it was just a little too long for me. I would have to remember to fix the straps when I had time today.

As soon as I saw my house in view, my instincts kicked in. I grabbed the key that was in our hiding spot and put it in the lock before running up the stairs. I saw my dad asleep on the couch and my mom seemed to be pacing in the kitchen. She seemed nervous, but I didn't have time to ask her about what was up. I tried to be as quiet as possible but knew since I was rushing I was bound to make some sort of noise.

As I searched through my bag to try and find it, I realized it wasn't there. I dumped my bag out and rummaged again just to make sure, but sat there dumbfounded. What do I do now? I remember putting it in my bag at one point, so where could I possibly keep it now? It wasn't with my backpack. It wasn't with my gym bag. Those were the main places I would ever go in this town. Where could I have put it?

I stared up at my alarm clock to see that I would be late for school even if I rode with my parents. I might as well make the most of it. I shook my head and realized that maybe Aaron had left it in the car. Maybe it fell out. The only place that I would find him would be at school. Slipping out of the house, I walked calmly to school, but as I grew closer, I became more anxious. Would this feeling ever go away?

I wasn't even sure what period it was when I stepped into the school, but hordes of students were in the hallways. Maybe it was a switch between classes. I could ask someone, but everybody either seemed to be rushing to their next class or just gossiping with their friends. I saw a couple of stares come towards me, but I ignored them. I was on a mission to find Aaron. This was harder than I would have thought though. I had only toured the school once before and it was only to get to my classes. I wasn't shown where my locker was nor was I shown where any extras like bathrooms, nurses, or offices were.

When I pulled out the school map and my schedule, I continued to walk. It was my fault. Why would I keep walking even if I was reading? Whatever my reasoning was, it didn't matter when I walked into someone and accidentally pushed them to the ground. The papers went to the ground with them and I was fearful that I would cause a scene. People stopped talking and the majority of the people stopped moving. When I looked to see who I accidentally pushed, I was relieved to see Aaron.

How convenient.

The people he was talking to seemed to vanish from sight and when he looked up, I saw panic and fear in his eyes. I instantly felt bad and crouched down to meet him. His books were scattered all in front of him and I reached over to help him gather them. The fear was now gone, but he still hadn't moved from the position on the ground. I slowly started to get up, but he didn't follow me. It was like he was paralyzed with fear.

"Do you have my necklace?" I asked. I scratched my head because I felt awkward as I towered over him. I was naturally taller than most people, but Aaron usually stood a bit taller than me. It was weird to have to look down to talk to him. He slowly pulled the necklace from his backpack and I felt anger build up inside of me. He did have it. I didn't even want to know how he had gotten it though. His hand shook as I grabbed it back and I whispered to him, "Don't ever touch this again."

"Tanner–"

"Don't talk to me." I looked down at him. He was slowly getting up from the push I gave him and I shook my head at him. "Ever again."

I abruptly got up from him and walked away. With the time I had remaining in this class period, I pushed myself to the bathroom. Once in the stall, I let a couple of deep, shaky breaths out before turning the pendant over in my hands. I would have to remember to get a chain for this. My mom would have one. Once my breathing became even, I slipped the pendant in my back pocket and splashed water in my face. Even from the noise in the bathroom, I could hear the warning bell go off to get to class.

I still didn't know what period it was. Should I go out of my comfort zone and ask someone? Should I just randomly show up to a class and ask what period it was? I know they had teachers monitoring the halls to help lost students. How embarrassing would that be though? I couldn't imagine doing that. I shook my head and knew that I couldn't just stay in the bathroom all day. I'm sure my mom got a call that I was late for school.

I probably made a great first impression. People would think that I was a bully. I just hoped nobody would try to challenge that and realize I was a fraud. I just wanted my necklace back. It had sentimental value to it and I didn't even mean to push him. I hope he knew that.

After finally getting out of the bathroom, I tried to look for my locker. When I started finding locker numbers close to what mine was, I was easily able to find mine. There wasn't any lock on it so I was a little sketched out, but relieved. For whatever reason, I could not get locks to work for me. I don't know if I don't turn it right enough or not left enough. They were always just a mystery to me. I stuffed my gym clothes in my locker and when I heard the bell for the classes ring, I was able to catch a glimpse of Luke.

At first, he was about to ignore me but stopped. He let his arm go of some girl he was with and she scurried off without him. I tried to keep my judgmental mind to myself, but he already had a girl into him? It was the first day of school. He looked at the paper in my hands and pointed to the current period we were at. He led the way for me and I have never been so grateful for him.

"You look like shit," he told me as he showed me the door to my class.

I smiled appreciatively at him as he disappeared into his class. I knocked politely on the door and felt self-conscious again. I grabbed the pendant from my back pocket and started fiddling with it in my hand. Luke knows how to make a girl feel self-conscious. I don't know how he got all of the other girls to fall for him. Unless it was different because I was his sister.

As soon as I entered the room, I was handed a pink slip without any instruction. I blushed red but took an empty seat anyway. Upon closer inspection, I noticed that there was nothing written on it. Was it valid then? Or were they just trying to make a point? I listened to a little bit of what was being said but zoned out when she began taking roll. My back immediately straightened when I heard Aaron's name being called.

I stared back at him and he saw me. His face darkened a bit and he turned to face the class. I watched him a little bit and noticed that no one was sitting near him. Every table around him was empty. Feeling a bit bad, I bit my lip and swiveled in my chair. I didn't think

Aaron was disliked so much that no one would sit next to him.

"Chloe?" I must've zoned out for a while because she didn't even say my last name. I huffed and cautiously raised my hand. "Oh, my little delinquent." I furrowed my eyebrows and she refused to meet my gaze.

I zoned out for the rest of the class though. It was like every other beginning of school year activity; ice breakers, handing out books, rules and expectations, and syllabus day. I stopped listening and when I zoned back in, it was time for the next class. In the halls, I didn't talk to anyone or go to my locker. I was able to find the next class with a breeze and found that Aaron was in this class as well. I was surprised and while I walked towards him, I forced myself to walk right by him.

I needed to make new friends.

"Chloe?"

I looked up with a smile on my face but it faltered when I saw our teacher taking attendance.

A male teacher.

Chapter Four

"It's alright," the teacher said, cleaning up the mess that was on the floor. I watched as other students walked out of the room without offering to help him and huffed when I realized that I would have to. I picked up some of the items that had scattered around the room and handed them to him. It was my fault anyway. I had pushed my chair right into him which caused him to drop everything. Why did he have to walk so close behind me? There was enough room for him to walk without needing to be near me. " Are you coming to do extra credit today?"

I stopped picking up things and had to think of an excuse. If I denied his help, he might call my parents about my grades. If I accepted his help, he might make me feel uncomfortable again. My mom always told me if someone made me uncomfortable, to not be alone with them.

"Uh, yeah," I replied.

I handed him the rest of his things before scurrying off in the hallway. He seemed satisfied with my answer and didn't register the hesitation in my voice. I knew that I was going to be late for my next class even if I sprinted so when I saw Luke, I stopped to chat anyway. Luke could help me out of the predicament I was in. He could be the person who helps me. I trusted him.

"Luke!" I yelled once he was within hearing range.

"Hm?"

I wanted the conversation to be private, but it didn't look like the people Luke was with would be leaving. While some of his friends parted when I came around, the girl by his side held on tighter. It didn't look like she would be leaving. Luke didn't refocus his attention on me and instead kept staring at the girl. Did he know that I was here? He always seemed to have someone at his side and it was annoying that I couldn't keep his attention off of them. If I didn't need to talk to him so urgently, I wouldn't mind. I only minded now because he was distracted. I needed his attention. It was even more distracting because this was a girl that Luke had been trying to win over for a long time. He would definitely want to keep her entertained for a week before he dumped her.

"Can you stay after school with me?" I pleaded. He thought for a moment and looked at the girl by his side. "I need a ride and..." It was clear that I was thinking up an excuse on the spot. Luke pretended not to notice, but I could see from the glint in his eye that he knew. "The teacher wanted to see you too."

I gulped and waited for Luke's final answer. He looked at the girl by his side and then at my pleading face before deciding that he would. It felt like so much pressure had lifted off of my shoulders. For the first time in a long time, I hugged him goodbye. I said goodbye to

him and the girl by his side and waddled off to my next
class. I quickly texted him the information about where to
go and when and he replied with a smiley face.

No more awkward uncomfortable silence with that
teacher.

***

"I need my schedule changed," I blurted out. The school
counselor blinked her eyes at me as if I stuttered. She was
probably surprised that I disturbed the peaceful
environment. I sat down on one of the chairs she had
without permission. I needed her full attention and for her
to realize how serious the situation was. I closed the door
behind me and hoped that no one could hear the
conversation we were having. I hoped that she didn't
think I was being rude though. To me, this was an
emergency. "I need my third-period and eighth-period
class changed." She looked towards the paper in my hand
and immediately began to ponder over what to ask me. "I
don't think they'll fulfill my learning ability." That was a
lie, but she didn't need to know that.

"Oh?" It took her a moment to put her tea down
and access her computer. Once on, she clicked some keys
on her computer and looked down at my paper. "And why
is that? Too fast? Too slow?"

"I've had a similar class last year," I whispered.
She looked over at me as if she didn't believe me but it
also may have been that I started whispering. I was loud

and a bit rude when I first walked in. Now I needed to get what I wanted so I knew to be respectful and lower my tone with her.

"I won't be able to change your third period," she mentioned. "Looking at your prior transcripts, you have had American Literature, but not world Literature which is what we have you currently in." She gazed at the computer longer. "Unfortunately, we do not have any openings in the other classes." She looked again at the schedule to double-check and I felt my cheeks turning hot. "Your eighth period is extracurricular so I will be able to change that. Do you know what you would like?"

I shook my head and she excused herself from her office. When she came back, she had a binder full of extra classes for me to take. I started going through them and made sure to look at the current instructors. The first female teacher I saw, I immediately picked her class. I held my breath when she started clicking her fingers on the keyboard. I was hoping that this class wasn't full.

"Excellent, by tomorrow you'll be in Driver's Ed." I smiled slightly and waited for my new schedule to be printed out. When I heard the printer stop making noise, the counselor carefully took it off and handed it to me. I looked down to see that all of my classes were female except for my third-period class. I was a bit disappointed that I couldn't get that class changed but she was able to help me with my other class.

Too bad, I loved the art class.

When I was done in her office, I walked towards the detention room. As soon as I had gotten there, I handed my pink slip in and gave my name. I was pointed to a seat and sat down near other students. Nobody talked as I passed and most of them kept their gaze to the ground. I noted that I probably shouldn't look at anyone else then. I needed to blend in, not stick out. Other students were scurrying into the room after me so as some of them passed me, I kept my head down too.

"She's the girl who beat up Aaron."

I wanted to shrivel into my clothes. As a new student, any gossip about you was going to be part of your reputation from there on out. I never really made headlines unless it was that people were finding out there was a new girl. Now I had to worry if people thought I was a bully. I didn't mean to run into Aaron and I hoped that Aaron knew that. He was bullied enough and didn't need to think that I was out to get him too. The more I thought about it, the angrier I felt myself get. I have never been pictured as a violent person in any of my past schools. I didn't want anybody to be afraid of me.

If this is what everyone was thinking about me, then I felt really bad. I knew that Aaron was often bullied at school. Missy had let it slip once or twice that he was there so he could learn to defend himself. It wouldn't help his reputation if people were spreading that he was beaten up by a girl either. Even though Aaron and I both knew that girls and boys could equally fight, it didn't mean our classmates did. A common stereotype was that girls were weaker than boys.

My mind wandered around about the possible topic until I was released from detention. At least when I go to boxing, I could explain the situation to Aaron if he needed it. While I wasn't looking forward to that, I would be excited to box. I would explain to him what had happened and he would hopefully acknowledge it. I would explain that I didn't have my necklace and I grew frantic - first-day jitters. He knew that it was sentimental to me. The only part of me that wanted to go was the part that enjoyed boxing. It was a great way for me to relieve the stress, fear, and anger I had from today.

I rushed to my locker to grab my gym clothes out of it. Along with that was my phone. I turned it on and took my time with getting all of my books organized so that I would be ready for tomorrow. When the phone lit up, I watched as a couple of text messages showed up. I was curious because usually, I only had game notifications.

The ones from Missy were the only ones that caught my eye. My eyes scanned the texts multiple times until I couldn't see the screen because of how blurry my vision was getting. Tears appeared in the corner of my eyes and threatened to spill over. Once again, I felt anger bubble up inside of me. She banned me from boxing at the gym for the entire week. Somehow she had heard the news that I had fought Aaron. I'm not sure if she had heard it from him or someone else but either way, it was untrue. Why would Aaron lie about that? Did he think I meant to push him to the ground? The only bright side was that she would allow me to come in tomorrow and work. If I worked a little bit, she would allow me to box. It was a fair trade-off and I knew she needed help around the gym. Maybe the punishment was only this severe because she wanted my help.

For today, I had to make a decision on how to help with my anger. I was afraid that I wouldn't be able to control it. The only thing that has ever helped me with my anger was boxing and now that it was taken away from me for a day, I might lose it. I've tried other things such as writing in a journal, exercising, reading, and others but nothing works for me. I wasn't sure if it was because I got to hit something and that was my outlet for anger, but nothing could compare to it. Maybe it was the subtle pain I had felt from it. Like I was punishing myself for feeling these things.

Not only was I mad at myself for running into Aaron, but I was mad at Aaron. We were the only boxers from this school. I only knew that because most of the patrons were adults or college-aged students. The only person who could have known about the fight was Aaron. Why would Aaron lie about it? He would have to know that I didn't mean to run into him.

I put my phone away into my pocket and carefully organized everything that I would need to take home. As soon as my foot stepped out onto the pavement of the sidewalk, I started running home. I refused to take any breaks and my lungs were screaming at me to stop. I kept pushing through until I finally got home. I have never felt the burn in my lungs to be as powerful as they were now. I coughed and choked on the air that was rushing in and out before finally going into my room. While that helped a little bit, it didn't compare to what boxing had let me do. I would argue that it was my second favorite thing to do after the running. Maybe music would help me too. I often listened to it while I was working out. Maybe it could be my third way to let out anger. I smiled to myself and shut the lights off as my music began to play. I just need to calm myself - breathe in, breathe out, breathe in, breathe out. I ended up so relaxed that when my eyelids became heavy, I couldn't fight to stay awake.

I fell into a mixture of reality and a mixture of nightmares.

All truth.

***

I listened as the final bell rang for the end of school and silently opened my locker. While I felt like I was quiet, everyone around me felt louder than ever. I clutched the necklace that was around my neck and placed my backpack into the cramped lockers. It barely fit but it would work momentarily. Conversations and laughter started to disappear down the hall towards cars and busses, but I walked the opposite way. Searching the halls for my brother, I was disappointed to see that he wasn't anywhere I could find. I checked near my lockers, his lockers, and anywhere that he might hang out to wait for me. Maybe he was upstairs already?

When no additional students were roaming the hallways, I found myself wandering up the stairs. I did it slowly just in case I could catch Luke. He wouldn't bail on me. When I turned the corner to my teacher's room, I was surprised to see that he wasn't up here either. I bit my lip, slowed my walk, and kept staring behind me. Could he still be downstairs?

"Chloe?"

I turned around at the sound of my name. He had a pleasant smile on his face and he opened the door for me to come in. As if I needed his permission. I looked down the hall and checked behind me again but couldn't hear anybody coming. I looked back at him and he seemed puzzled for a second before I looked again.

"I'm waiting for someone."

I scratched my forehead and looked behind me again. The teacher also looked down the halls and walked around a bit. He shook his head and his face looked puzzled. He shrugged his shoulders and started heading into the classroom.

"It doesn't look like anyone's here, Chloe."

He waited outside of his door again and I bit my lip. I looked around once more and he walked timidly towards me. He seemed a little impatient with me so he grabbed me by the shoulders and pushed me inside of his room. I made sure to look around again but still could not *find Luke anywhere. He closed the door behind me and I forced myself into a seat far away from the front of the room. He went up to his desk and came back with a stack of papers and a red pen.*

I was relieved when he left me by the door. I slowly looked at all of the tests and began grading them. I tried not to look at the names that were on the sheets so I wouldn't be biased towards them. When it came down to me seeing my name on one of the tests, I froze. Was it possible for me to grade my test without being biased?

"Not going to cheat, are we?" the teacher asked. I flinched when he whispered behind me. He was so close to my body and I hadn't even realized that he had gotten up from his desk. It helped me feel better when I realized that he was joking. I would hope he wouldn't think that I would cheat. His amused smile on his face is what gave it away. He moved closer to me so that he could look over my shoulder. I didn't expect him to place his chin on my shoulder. When he did, my body stiffened. He made it worse by moving his arm next to me and pointing to a question that I had gotten wrong. I bit my lip to prevent any noise to come out and my frustration of getting an answer wrong, but I corrected it. He nodded his head and distanced himself from me.

As he started to go back to the front of the class, I finally felt myself breathe normally again. I grabbed the necklace I had around my neck and began to play with it as I graded tests. I eventually found a rhythm of grading again and when I was done with the stack, I turned around to see him watching me.

My body instantly reacted by leaning against the table behind me. I didn't realize he had moved again and found it freaky that he could move without being heard. He smirked at my reaction and I handed him the tests immediately.

"Uh, here are your tests," I replied.

He grabbed the tests out of my hand. He leafed through the tests for a second but stopped at one of them. He made a noise from his throat and scurried back to his desk. In interest, I followed him towards his desk and watched as he began putting digits in the computer's database. I felt my jaw drop when I noticed that he had placed a zero where I should've gotten a 95 at.

"What was that for?" I quietly asked.

"Cheating," he replied.

"Cheating? How did I cheat?"

"You didn't correct them right." He showed me the paper in his hands and I squinted my eyes at my paper but didn't notice any mechanical errors that I had made. "You marked your paper incorrectly while I was standing behind you, I saw."

"That's impossible," I said. I got closer to the desk and crouched down next to him. I felt my back stiffen when he placed a hand on my back and the other on my paper. He pointed to a specific problem with lots of eraser marks. "I did that before I saw the answer," I squeaked.

"So she says," he replied. I looked up at him and came nose-to-nose with him. I squeaked since he was too close to be comfortable. Losing my balance on my feet—since I was crouching—I began to fall backward. Thankfully, the teacher was there and managed to stop me from falling by placing both hands under my armpits.

"Thanks," I whispered. Letting myself get up, I soon realized that his grip has gotten tighter on me. "Uh, you can let go now."

"Chloe, can I ask you a question?"

"Once you let go of me.". He did so and let his hands fall. I sat down at a student desk and he followed me as well. He sat down next to me and showed interest in what he was saying. He didn't seem malicious anymore.

"Are you making any friends here?"

"Uh, everyone's nice but nobody is as good as my old friends." My back stiffened as he began to play with the sleeves on my long-sleeve shirt. I moved them away, but his hands followed the little distance they moved.

"Tell me about them."

"Summer was my best friend but she was severely disliked. People said she wasn't a very nice person but I believe they didn't understand sarcasm very well." I paused for a moment when he rolled my sleeve up. I was getting distracted and couldn't concentrate on what he was asking.

"And the other friend?"

"He was Tanner, my ex-boyfriend." Water rolled up in my eyes that I didn't even notice that he had started *combing his hand through my hair. I tried not to think about him because I needed to make myself happier. I wasn't sure what the normal length for mourning was, but I knew my parents were getting sad for me. Was there even a limit on how long you can mourn someone?*

"Why are you wearing a long-sleeve shirt during summer?"

"Laundry day," I dryly replied as he pinned my hair behind my neck. I let him do it and let tears roll down my cheeks. I wasn't sure if I was crying because I was thinking about Tanner or if I was uncomfortable with him. Could it be both?

"Was this Tanner important to you?"

"Very," I replied. Sensing that I couldn't concentrate when I was talking about Tanner, the teacher decided to put his hand on my knee, slowly crawling up to my thigh. "Tanner was the one who could put a smile on my face even in my ugliest moments."

"I don't think you're ugly," the teacher said. My brain immediately clicked on and I wiped any tears away from my eyes. Seeing that his hand was crawling up my leg, I shooed it away and leaned back against the seat as much as I could. "Everyone else does. Nobody thinks you're pretty. Nobody but me." I felt myself bite my lip and I slowly thought about it. Was he right? He was a teacher and could eavesdrop on others' conversations. "Your mother doesn't think you're pretty. Why else would she get you makeup?" He placed the palm of his hand on my cheek and I bit my lip, still uncomfortable. Was he

right? *"Your father thinks you're disgusting. Isn't that why you moved once Tanner died? He didn't think you deserved him."* I slowly let more tears fall down my cheeks. Why was he saying this to me? He was just being so nice and now he's hurting my feelings. *"Are you okay?"*

"No." I shook my head and let him hug me. I even hugged back—not thinking of the consequences. I felt his hands fall down my back but it was shaking so hard, I thought it was an accident. *"I just miss Tanner so much."*

"Um-hmm." He patted my back and slowly began to reach towards my thighs. Not wanting to startle me, he stopped right on my lower back and rubbed, getting lower. I shuddered so hard with tears that I didn't even notice when his hands made their way to the place where only gum packets should be.

I didn't notice.

Once I was able to calm myself down, I started leaning back for the chair and accidentally brought him back with me. He excused himself and we sat uncomfortably for a moment. I removed his hands from my waist and pulled my shirt back down so my bare skin wasn't showing anymore. His hands felt weird when they touched my skin. They were too rough.

"That's all right, you have me," he said. He scooched his chair closer to mine and before I knew it, he was stroking my neck with his finger.

"S-stop," I tried.

"Don't act like you don't want it," he snarled back. I stiffened and wondered what happened to his soothing voice. "You're the one who advanced to me while hugging me." He slowly breathed in and placed his lips on my neck. His breath was warm.

"Stop, please," I pleaded.

He didn't. He progressed to the point where his hands made their way up to my bra. He reached his hand behind my back and attempted to unhook it. I was crying and I was shuddering. I knew now that I was crying because of him. While Tanner was a sore spot in my brain, I felt safe when talking about him. I wanted him to stop but he was taller and heavier than me. I couldn't do anything and my brother was nowhere around me. Could I fight back? What if he changed my grades to failing ones? My family would kill me.

"Don't worry," he whispered in my ear. "You have the marks to prove you enjoyed it." He placed his lips back on my neck and I could feel him biting at it. Once he got my bra undone, I immediately got up. I forced my legs up and rapidly moved away from him.

He didn't react and stayed seated.

I rushed out without thinking about anything. I didn't wander the school and I didn't look for my brother. I immediately rushed home. We only lived five minutes away so it wasn't a long walk. It gave me enough time to fix my hair so they were covering the slight bruises on my neck. I also managed to fix my bra so that I was secure again. Even though I felt safe again, I still wanted to cry.

Where was my brother?
He promised to be there.
Where was he?

Chapter Five

"No fighting today, Tanner!" Missy yelled at me. I bit the inside of my cheek and began walking away from the punching bags. I was hoping to sneak in some exercise before I had to work. She knew me so well. If she knew me as well as I think she would, she knew that I was in a bad mood today, and having her keep telling me what I can and cannot do was annoying me. I know it was her job, but I just wanted the relief. "Tanner, you're on probation."

I opened my mouth but closed it once I saw Missy raise her eyebrows. If you talked back to her, she would put you in your place. I didn't feel like dealing with that type of Missy today. I didn't want to be banned from her gym. Then I would have to find a new place and who knows what their policies would be? Who knows if they would even accept me? Would my mom or dad be able to afford something new?

"That's right Tanner, you better shut your mouth."

I bit my tongue so hard that I started to feel a metallic taste form. I released the tension when I realized it had to be blood that I was drawing with my teeth. As she said my name, I saw some spectators watching me for a show. Would I pick a fight with the boss? I'm sure that they are all experienced enough to know that Missy could hold her ground. They probably assumed I was dumb enough to try and challenge her. I wasn't though. I knew my place in this gym. I knew that it was Missy's way or the highway.

Instead, I put my stuff on a bench. Since the gym was covered in mirrors, I was able to catch my reflection in one of them. Subtly, I started to check myself out. I rolled my sweatpants down to just above the yoga shorts I was wearing under them. This led me to see my abs and I couldn't help but flex them.

"Seriously Tanner?"

Apparently, I was not as subtle as I thought I was.

After the embarrassment of getting caught had worn off of me, I turned to face Aaron. I was shocked to see him without a shirt on. He always stood tall over me, but without a shirt, he looked muscular. The shirts he wore were probably two sizes too big. He drowned in them and they made him seem like he was a twig. Without the shirt, I could see just how toned he was.

He was hot.

As I continued to look at his body, my eyes eventually made it up to his face. He was smirking because he knew he had caught me looking. However, I didn't pay attention to that for too long. My gaze fell upon a black eye he had. I gawked for a second, but my eyes turned back to his body. He must've gotten that black eye from a bully. If we would just wear more form-fitting shirts, I'm sure he wouldn't be bullied as much. He could show them that he could kick their asses.

"This?" He pointed to the bruise and I gulped wondering what he was going to say. His voice was more aggressive than I have ever heard him use for me. He usually spoke in a hushed voice or whisper. "This is from you. Not directly." He grabbed his water bottle and started drinking from it before he put his shirt back on. "Don't worry though, I'm on probation too."

"W-Why?" I asked. He pointed to his bruised eye and slightly smiled at me. "D-Did I do that t-to you?" I asked. I already knew the answer was no but I didn't want Aaron to think that I didn't care enough to ask. Besides, he just explained it to me. I didn't directly give him it.

In response to my question, he began to chuckle which increased to a full-on laugh. I was stunned for a moment at what he was implying and then couldn't help but groan and clench my hands into fists. Aaron looked down and smirked even wider. I needed to explain to him that I didn't mean to push him in the hall. I have never used my boxing on anyone to hurt them. Why would I start with him? Would he even believe me?

"I would be able to ta-ta-ta-ta-take you." At first, I didn't quite get the drift that he was mocking me until the moment when he sneered at me. "We all know that stutter is fake, Tanner."

He walked past me and purposely hit my shoulder against his. I stood still for a moment and felt my body tremble all at once. Why was he being so mean to me now? He knows what it's like to be bullied, so why is he doing it to me? Nobody has ever outrightly made fun of my stutter either. That was a new low from anybody. I didn't even hurt him on purpose! He had to know that I didn't shove him, I collided with him. I looked down at my body and then grabbed the necklace around my neck. It had a new chain on it now, but it felt a little awkward. It hung a little lower on my chest than I was used to but I thanked my mom regardless because it was the closest size to what I had before. Despite how appreciative I was for it, it still felt off to wear like this. I knew that I shouldn't wear it anyway. I walked towards the locker rooms with it held in my palm. This was my comfort piece, but maybe I needed to put it away. I was so desperate to feel the familiarity with it and to have Tanner with me, that I had caused Aaron to get hurt. I had accidentally hurt Aaron and other people had hurt him because of them thinking I had. I placed it in my bag with the wish that maybe if I used it less, I wouldn't be desperate for it. Although I knew the real reason wasn't because of the necklace itself. The real reason was because of me and the way I've been acting. Maybe Aaron being mean to me was an eye-opener of what I was acting like.

Grunting, I left the locker room and met up with him to understand what we were doing. We walked to an area restricted to workers only and slowly descended down some stairs into a basement. It was similar to a small laundry mat. There were washing machines, drying machines, folding areas, laundry baskets, and more. Aaron took a step towards the laundry and I looked at the washers. I guess I could start there. As I began thinking of reasons why Aaron was in here, I soon realized that he wasn't on probation—he was in here because that's how he got to come in here free. He paid his way through to boxing. Why would he lie to me about that though? I already knew the truth about him.

"Aaron, I'm sorry," I whispered. I threw a couple of towels in the washer and started the load. I had my back to Aaron so I couldn't see his reaction but I froze when I heard his footsteps coming towards me. I turned around and when I realized how close he was to me, I pressed my body against the washer I was working with. I hated when people got close to me.

He was smiling friendly at me and any meanness that was directed towards me earlier was gone. I shuddered as he was taller than me and was slightly more muscular than what I pictured him as. Realizing that I was uncomfortable, he backed up a few steps and stared at me intently. I crossed my arms over my stomach and wished that I would've put my shirt on before I came down here with him. Should this be where I confess to him that it wasn't intentional?

"What's so important about that necklace, anyway?" he asked. My body froze and I thought I misheard him. When he asked again, I felt my face crumble.

I was about to break down.

In front of Aaron.

I've only been asked that once and it didn't end well for me. I usually have boxing to calm me down but some memories just don't go away. Some betrayals don't go away. Some people don't go away.

Nothing goes away.

"Tanner?" I nodded my head to dismiss the subject and instantly went back to the beeping washer. I quietly put the detergent in the machine and closed the lid on it. I didn't want to face him as I placed my hands on top of it as it purred to life. I took a moment to collect my thoughts and turned around to see what Aaron was doing. Thankfully, he had gone back to his work and for some reason, I felt like I could trust him.

I didn't even trust Luke.

I didn't even trust my dad.

I didn't even trust myself anymore.

"It's my ex-boyfriend's," I whispered. I watched as Aaron stopped working for a moment to register my comment. He grabbed the powder detergent from the shelf like I didn't just spill a secret with him. He didn't ignore it completely though. He nodded his head a couple of times before making me smile with a simple one-word answer.

"Cool."

He wasn't being nosy like normal people would. He didn't want to know every detail. He must've known it was personal to me since he was so delicate with asking the questions. And for the remainder of the time we were on probation together, he didn't ask another question about the necklace to me. We did banter and joke around and it felt normal. I felt normal.

"That's it, Tanner." I nodded my head and looked towards the drier, which was still humming with life. "Missy will get it later." I jumped off of the washer that I had my rear planted on and felt the sweat slide off of my stomach and down my legs. There was no air conditioning in this part of the building. "You get used to it."

I nodded my head and was the first to go up the stairs. When I noticed that Aaron wasn't following me, I became curious. I snuck back down and peeked inside. He was standing in front of the washer again. That was strange. We had just finished all of the loads.

"A-Aaron?" I asked. He jumped and a white cloth flew to the floor. That wasn't a gym towel and I knew that for certain since we only had blue towels. "A-are you doing your o-own laundry here?" I asked. Aaron quickly ran up to me—causing me to freeze—and slammed the door shut. He swiped my body with his arm and moved me away from it. I was still frozen so my body just caved into his arm as he set me near the corner of the room. He took me to the farthest corner away from the door and my body was yelling for me to react.

"Please don't tell," he whispered. "I mean, I guess you could but I don't have time to do it at home." He looked around and ran back towards the washer. "I know that you must want to for revenge since I got you down here and that you missed boxing but—"

"A-are you having trouble at your h-house?" I whispered. Aaron's back stayed straight and I was sure that he heard me even though I had barely made a noise. I could tell that he was contemplating what he should tell me. I knew that no matter his answer, I would have to show him the same respect he showed me. I was nosey though so I would have to show a lot of self-control.

"No."

I nodded my head even though I didn't believe him. I made my way towards the door anyway and turned back to him as he was frantically moving everything at lighting speed so he wouldn't be caught again. I watched for a second and knew that they were all of his clothes. I don't know how I didn't see the laundry basket before, but it looked like weeks worth of stuff.

"And I had a really good time down here." I blinked as I opened the door and was flooded with heavy lighting. I looked over at Aaron and he was kneeling on the dirty ground and wasn't moving. He was motionless as he pretended to move clothes from the dryer to his bag. "With you," I whispered.

Chapter Six

"Where are you going, all dolled up?" Luke asked me. I turned around with a smile on my face and was attempting to put a hoop in my ear. "What's with your hair?" I turned around back to the mirror and looked at my fishtail braid. I quickly gave him a disgusted look—I was purposely going for the messy look. He would never understand what was currently in right now anyway. He simply didn't care about it.

"Tanner is getting adopted soon," I replied. "And he invited me to celebrate with his family." I looked towards Luke and saw his smile grow. This was the first relationship I have ever had. It meant a lot to me to have his support and the rest of my family's support. They welcomed him into the house before I announced that we were dating. It felt wonderful to not have to worry that they didn't like him. "Decisions." I looked into my closet to try and figure out what I wanted to wear now. I heard Luke scoff but I also heard him 'fall' onto my bed. "My leather pants—"

"No."

I rolled my eyes and threw the pants towards the ground. "Yoga or skinny?"

"Why are you going tight today?"

"Skinny it is," I whispered while avoiding his question. I undressed my pants and quickly tugged the

skinnies on. Luke rolled his eyes at me and darted until I gave him the signal that I was dressed. "I'm not going for tight." I gestured towards my top and he shrugged his shoulders. "And I just thought that it would be better if I wore something that wasn't me."

"But isn't that why Tanner fell for you in the first place?" Luke asked. I shrugged my shoulders and pulled my converse on. "I need to give him a talk before you go out with him."

"And his family," I reminded. "But don't threaten him too much." I smiled at Luke's protectiveness and I opened the door. We raced down the stairs and met at the landing. I quickly turned the TV on and plumped my butt on the couch.

"No!" Luke yelled, jumping on top of me. He grabbed the remote from my hands stopped me from putting on my comfort movie and turned on the cartoons. I licked my lips and shrugged my shoulders at him, it didn't matter to me since I would be leaving soon. I just had to wait for the honk of the horn and I knew that I would be out the door.

As I waited, I heard some loud sobbing coming from the kitchen. Luke and I shot each other a look of worry but remained in our seats. I wished Tanner would hurry up and get here so I could have a good night for most of the night. My mom didn't cry often, but when she did, it was a serious issue. I wanted to know after I celebrated with Tanner and his family. I just wanted a good night. Was that selfish of me?

"Chloe! Luke!"

Luke and I immediately started rushing towards the kitchen. However, I stopped in my tracks when I heard a knock at the door. I looked back at him and he nodded his head as if he approved of me going to the door instead. When he stopped and did a double-take, I forced myself to stare too. Red and blue flashing lights were in my driveway. When I heard the knock again, I cautiously opened the door to see a police officer there.

"Are you Chloe Duff?" he asked. I nodded my head and looked back at Luke. He shrugged his shoulders and I watched as my dad came from the kitchen. He shook his head for me to continue listening and I saw tears running down his face. He never cried. "Do you know Tanner Kemp?" I nodded my head again and felt more tears running down my cheeks. This could only mean one thing and I doubt it was good. I looked towards Luke who stayed frozen in the hallway. Slowly, his face started to crumble and he hung his head for a second. He must've known what was coming next since he put a hand on my shoulder and apologized to me. "We're so sorry to say that Tanner Kemp was pronounced dead at..." He said some other things that I wasn't aware of and I just blinked. He kept talking and when I focused back on him, he looked concerned. "Ma'am?"

"Hm?" I asked.

"Are you alright?" I nodded my head calmly and closed the door on the officer nicely.

Luke seemed worried for me but he didn't do anything. He watched as I kicked off my shoes and then slowly walked up the stairs. I didn't cry. I didn't scream. I didn't think. I didn't speak. I didn't believe it. I didn't hope.

I didn't sleep.
I didn't love.
I didn't...

***

"Thanks, mom," I said. She kissed my forehead as she headed out of my room. She had a long day of work ahead of her since she hasn't been going the past two days. She didn't have time to investigate my wolf-cry of feeling sick. Right before closing the door, she looked back at me with disbelief. I know that she doesn't trust me when I said that I was sick. However, she didn't challenge me on it either. She didn't feel my forehead or take my temperature. She knew what today really was. I didn't feel like facing the rest of the world and telling everyone that I'm miserable. I was in a bad mood and would take it out on everyone. I didn't want to have to explain it to them.

"Luke will take care of you," she whispered as she closed the door. I shut my eyes at his name and hoped she wasn't being serious. I didn't want anybody home with me today, especially Luke. I just wanted one day by myself. Why couldn't he go out with his friends? Or go to his girlfriend's house? Or just be anywhere but home?

I remained in my bed and started feeling around for my necklace. I sighed when I realized I wasn't wearing it. I left it in my gym bag and I wasn't even sure I wanted to wear it today. It's just something that comforts me. I feel like it would just bring up more sad memories for me today though. I laid my hand on my chest in defeat and started biting the inside of my cheek instead. Another reason that I chose to fiddle with the necklace.

I was too rung up in my thoughts that I didn't even flinch when a knock was at my door. I just let Luke knock and then jiggle my door, to find out that mom had locked it. I smiled and silently thanked my mom for remembering how I liked things. I didn't like people coming and going as they pleased as it felt like it broke my privacy. My family understood that if I needed them, I would ask. They understood I was growing older and might not want them to walk in on me.

"Tanner?" Luke asked. I rolled onto my stomach and planted my face into my pillow. I didn't want to hear what he had to say to me. Today was my day and I didn't want Luke with me. "Are you okay?" he asked. I grunted in response to him and I listened to the noise outside of my door. It sounded like he laid against my door instead of giving up. Usually, he just went and minded his own business. Maybe he was actually concerned for me. "We all know what you're doing."

There it was. The accusation in his voice. I guess it wasn't so much of an accusation if he was correct in his assumption. I knew what I was doing. I was hoping nobody else would realize the date though. At least he called me out on it though. It resembled the bickering we used to have before I completely retracted from him. Before I lost all of my trust in him.

"You know it's only about six hours away, we could go without mom or dad finding out," Luke finally said. I stood puzzled for a moment but didn't object to what he was talking about. "Just so you know, everyone else is grieving too but we were all going to ignore what the date was. We were going to pretend as nothing happened." He paused and I stayed staring at the door. "Mom and dad have succeeded at it so far. I shuddered a little when I realized what today was, so I can never imagine what you're going through."

I huffed as I realized that he wasn't going to leave me alone as I wanted. Today was the day that my life took a turn for the worst. After this day two years ago, something bad has always happened to me. I have lost my boyfriend and shortly afterward lost my best friend. I moved and that year was the worst of them all. The first day here, I get put into detention and people also think I'm a bully. I felt tears brim in my eyes.

Today was the day that Tanner died.

The day my life started going downhill.

I immediately unlocked my door and sprinted past Luke. He was dazed for a moment but quickly got up after me. He was yelling something after me but I wasn't listening. I wanted to take Luke's suggestion of going back to our last home. I just didn't want Luke with me. If anything, I could hitchhike or try to take a bus.

It was only six hours by car.

If anything, I could probably walk for four days and eventually get there. I wasn't sure how to get there, but that was what phones were for. What if my phone died on the way there though? I shook my head at the thought. Was I planning on traveling by foot? I was determined and my determination was stronger than anything else I had. Stronger than the loss of Tanner, stronger than the agony of the incident, and stronger than the love for my brother.

"Tanner!" I was surprised to hear my brother's voice again and I silently wished he would run out of breath and collapse. "Tanner, get in the car." I looked over at Luke and felt an eery creep over to me. How did I not hear his car? I thought he was running to stay caught up with me. Luke may be attractive and fit, but he was not athletic. I contemplated my thoughts for a second before hopping into the car.

"To Tanner's?"

"To Tanner's."

Chapter Seven

As I walked into the school as a new student, I felt all eyes that were on me and saw the judgmental looks from them. I was shocked to see that my outfit didn't look like any of theirs. The girls were all wearing sweatpants with their hair in loose buns with no makeup on. I was wearing my tight pants with a button-down shirt. The students at the last school I attended often wore something similar to what I was wearing. It was weird to see how different schools were from each other. Some schools had uniforms. Some schools had dress codes Some had neither. I would have to take note of this school's trends. I didn't want to stick out and just wanted to become another face in the crowd. After people stared at me, I could tell that their mouths were dropping at the sight of my brother right next to me. He would coyly pretend that I wasn't related to him and we would walk into the office together. After we were given our schedules, we both sat down for a moment and spoke to each other in a way only we could understand.

"Right?" Luke asked.

"Right," I said, nodding. I could see the stares of the receptionist but we communicated more with our facial expressions and body language. It was like we had a secret language that only we knew about. "Just don't break any hearts today, Luke."

He smiled at me and then stood up. He ruffled my hair before walking out of the office. I waited a couple more minutes to walk out after him because that was just our code. He would walk out first and then when he was far enough away, I would come out too. I didn't want to be compared to him like I often was. We were different people. We had different interests. I didn't want to be known as his little sister and he didn't want to be known as my older brother. We were tired of the comparisons.

I would hate being a twin.

Staring at my schedule as I made my way down the hall, I couldn't help but hear the muffled sounds of yelling coming from close by. I looked around to see that nobody else was reacting to the noise and for a moment, I thought I had imagined it. As I stood still in the hallways and people had to maneuver their way around me, I couldn't hear anything besides the laughs and squeals of everyone seeing their best school friend again. I walked away thinking it was nothing and went to find my locker. Maybe it was a noise from someone's phone.

When I found the locker, I was instantly discouraged from using it. There was a group of kids on the surrounding lockers and they didn't seem like they were going to move. They were chatting blissfully about how their summers went and then the girls were comparing each other's first day of school outfits. I scoffed knowing that I would probably never have access to my locker if I was surrounded by the cliché group of kids. At least nobody was making out in front of it this time.

"Guys!" I heard someone yell. I looked over to see a fit guy with sandy hair and the blue eyes that every girl wants. I darted my eyes to the floor when he looked towards me and I could sense that the corners of my lips were tugging upwards. "This girl needs to get to her locker!" Everyone stopped talking and looked over at me and I felt a huge blush creep onto my cheeks. "Thank you!" he said.

As the crowd parted, I found my locker number and silently opened it. It was a mess. There was graffiti on the door of it and the hooks for a hoodie were missing while the top shelf was bent and broken. I sighed and looked at how the walls of my locker were bending too. I swiftly threw my jacket in and attempted to escape as the students started to crawl around the door again. I didn't even resist when I felt someone grab my wrist and pull me away. I just followed them. I didn't even notice it was the same boy who helped me before until we were on the other side of the hall. He was smiling down at me and I nodded my head in appreciation.

Looking down at my paper, I ignored him and attempted to find my way to my next class. I didn't care that he was following me and looking over my shoulder. I couldn't tell why he was being nice to me. At the other schools, I have been to, if someone was nice to you it was because they wanted something from you.

"That's upstairs," he said. I looked at his eyes and nodded. "Here's a tip, anything starting with a two, means it's upstairs. Anything beginning with a one is downstairs."

"Thanks," I whispered.

Permitting myself to leave him, I did and realized that the bell had rung. I knew that most teachers were lenient for people being late to their class. They would have to know that I was new as well and they should probably expect it. I followed slowly and could hear the banging and rattling of what I did before. Following the noise, since the hall has now cleared out, I found myself in front of the janitor's closet.

I attempted to push the door but I knew it was wrong when I felt the lunge of the door. The noise on the other end became quiet and I pulled the door outward towards me. As soon as I opened it, I squinted my eyes and was startled when a girl came out and slammed it shut.

She was of medium height and she looked around my age. The only thing odd about her was that she was dressed as a five-year-old. She had the Dorothy dress on from The Wizard Of Oz and her hair was braided into pigtails. I stood astounded at her until she started speaking to me.

"Thank you, so much!" she gushed. She motioned for me to follow her and I did just that in fear that she would hate me if I didn't. Once we were inside the girls'

bathroom, she shut the main door and locked it tightly.
Was she even allowed to do that?

Once she looked in her reflection, she let her hair
out of the braided pigtails and teased her hair. I watched
in silence and she didn't speak until she was done with
her hair.

"I know we just met and everything, but do you
have pants or shorts I could wear?" she asked. I shook
my head and she pushed her lips to the side of her face. I
must've had a puzzled look on my face because
immediately when she turned to me, she explained what
she was doing. "My mom likes to dress me and won't let
me leave if I wear something she doesn't like."

"Do you know what you're going to do?" I
whispered. She stayed still for a moment and then nodded
her head with a slight shake. She brought her phone out
of her pocket and then texted someone. When she got the
notification back, she smiled. "They're on their way. I'm
Summer. You don't look familiar, are you new here?"

"Yeah, I'm Chloe." I smiled at her and she hugged
me. I was taken back for a minute but when she smiled, I
was reassured that it was just a genuine hug. I didn't like
physical affection so I hoped she wouldn't continue to do
that.

"If you hadn't opened the door for me, I would've
been stuck in there until the janitor came in."

"Why were you there in the first place?"

"People don't like me." She shrugged her
shoulders and brought out a lip balm. She smoothed it

against her lips and then popped the lips out. *"I don't let that bother me because now I have two friends."*

"Me and who else?" I asked. I assumed that we were friends but I didn't want to push my luck since I had just met her. How embarrassing would that be if she meant someone else was her friend? I immediately started blushing at my possible mistake and hoped that she wouldn't notice.

"Wait." Summer turned towards me and looked me dead in the eye. *"You actually want to be my friend? After I told you that no one likes me?"* I nodded my head in confusion and she seemed just as puzzled as I was. *"You do know what that can do to your social life, right?"*

"What social life?" I sarcastically asked. At first, I thought that I had offended Summer since she wasn't responding but soon she playfully punched me in the shoulder and smiled. We stood in a comfortable silence until the door was knocked on and Summer let someone in.

I was surprised to see the genuinely nice boy who had helped me earlier. He seemed stunned to see me too because we just stared at each other for a couple of moments.

"Who's this, Summer?"

Since Summer was already in the stall undressing, she couldn't see that we barely knew each other. She couldn't even sense that his voice cracked when he spoke. *"That's Chloe! She's my other friend and guess what,*

Tanner?" I arched my eyebrows. "She speaks in our native tongue!"

My eyebrows dipped down my face and I'm sure that I looked odd since I was staring at him too. So from what I know, he's incredibly fit and he was eye candy. From what Summer had just told me, they were misfits and were best friends. I didn't know either of them spoke another language though. Once she came out of the stall, I noticed her dress lying on the floor. Her hair was wavy from the braids and she was wearing a white tank top with black basketball shorts. She looked as comfortable and I was jealous now that I was stuck in my skinny jeans.

"Sarcasm!" she answered enthusiastically.

***

As I got out of the car and entered my way into the solemn and quiet graveyard, I couldn't help but shiver when I realized how many gravestones there were. I have never been to a cemetery before and it was an experience I wouldn't want anybody to have. So many people have lost their lives—whether of old age or from someone else's problems. However, it was calming. Anybody visiting was here for a reason. To realize that I wasn't the only one suffering, made the pain a little more suitable and helped me a bit more knowing that someone has lost someone in their lives, whether important or not. It was unnerving to think that all of these graves were people at one point in time.

"You go," Luke said. I barely heard him as he was talking to me because I was too determined to find Tanner's gravestone. "I need to give you your space."

I continued reading the headstones as Luke stayed behind in the car. I was thankful for him for driving me here and allowing me to get some closure. Allowing me to spend this time as I wanted to. As I continued reading, I knew that it would feel impossible for me to find Tanner's headstone. Right before his funeral, my mom and dad had packed up our house and forced us to move. I never got to say my goodbyes to him or his family. That was probably the worst part for me. I wanted to say goodbye.

Looking back, that's what I would've changed. I probably looked like I didn't care about Tanner when he had died. It probably looked like Summer was more of a suitable girlfriend for him because she stayed and I wouldn't be surprised if she continually visited him week after week. I hope their family knew how much Tanner had meant to me. I hope they didn't think badly of me because of my mom's decisions. If they did, I would blame her. I know how selfish that is, but how selfish is it to not let me say goodbye? She never even asked me. I resent her for that.

When I finally spotted Tanner's dad, I knew that he would be somewhere around the gravestone too. I dusted off nearby stones and attempted to read the dirty inscription on them. After I was done with one full aisle of headstones, I must've looked like a lost puppy who had given up hope of ever getting home because I had a patrolling security guard come up and talk to me.

"I'm trying to find a specific headstone." My voice cracked when I ended my sentence and I felt like I couldn't keep talking. The security guard must've been a mother because she planted a reassuring smile on her face and a friendly hand on my shoulder. "And he's not near his father's."

"Well, what's his name? Maybe I could help."

"Tan-ner." My voice cracked bad and I could tell that I was going to cry if I even got a chance to say his last name. The guard nodded her head and we searched for a minute together. Once we cleared a whole section without finding the grave, she asked me for his last name. When I wouldn't give it, she left me to find it myself. I couldn't blame her, how would she be able to find someone without the last name?

Not giving up, I continued to look until I was sure that I had checked every headstone. I couldn't be sure because the cemetery wasn't taken care of very well and it seemed like they were never visited very often. I didn't let this get me sad though, I continued along until I reached the last row and searched for another area.

That's when I saw it.

A grave in his dad's row. It was on the other end of the path for visitors and it was by itself. It looked like more stones could be added later, but I hoped nobody would ever be near. As I got closer, I saw a candle next to it. It was recently lit but almost burned out. I moved it so that I wouldn't accidentally kick it or knock it over. When I got to the stone, I dusted the top of it off. I kneeled on the dirt and read what was written on it.

Tanner Kemp.

The perfect son, friend, and boyfriend.

And boyfriend.

Boyfriend.

I curled my back and let my arms snuggle themselves around my legs. My back was already screaming from not being in proper posture but I didn't care. I felt the tears falling down my face and quietly reread his headstone to myself.

"Hey," Luke said. He sat down next to me but I didn't look or talk to him. Luke read the headstone and attempted to smile. I could see that his mood was darkening from being here though. When I looked over at him, he was blurry, but I could see that he took notice of my reaction. I could tell that he was crying in the car. His hair was ruffled at the edges and his eyes looked pink and sensitive around the edges.

Neither of us mentioned our looks to each other as we stared at what was in front of us. Before he came along, I wanted to talk quietly to Tanner but I knew it was useless if Luke would be here because I didn't want him to see me cry more than I was. I didn't want him to hear my voice crack and I didn't want him to see how much it still hurt that Tanner was gone.

And the drunk driver didn't even spend a night in jail.

I tried to whisper something encouraging to Luke, but I wasn't sure if he heard me or not. My heart felt like it was breaking when I heard him start to sniffle. I looked over at him and saw that his back was moving rapidly and I could hear tiny whimpers of him trying to shut them off. Biting my lip, I didn't understand how to comfort my brother since I'd never really seen him cry before. It was very unusual for anyone in our house to ever cry because we all hated emotion. The most sensitive person in the house was my mom and we didn't have a good relationship with her to talk about our feelings. We were an independent family where none of us liked asking for help because we felt weak. I was raised that showing emotion was weak.

We weren't one of the families to brag about how we got an A+ on a project. We didn't celebrate birthdays as other families did. Instead of celebrating together, the birthday person got a whole day to themselves and they could sleep all day if they wanted. They got twenty dollars to order whatever they wanted and there would be a happy birthday once, and then it was over. Most families would scoff at the idea, but our family liked that idea. We liked being alone.

We liked being anti-social.

At first, I was never like my family and neither was Luke. Luke was the guy everybody wanted to be around at school but if they saw him at home, they wouldn't want anything to do with him. And me. I was a social butterfly nerd that was told to crawl back in her cocoon and she did because she was afraid of being hated. We both wore a mask so that people wouldn't think we were weird. Luke loved being around people, but when he was home he liked to be by himself. I think he was afraid that he could only keep the mysterious persona up for so long before they found out that he was just a normal guy. Luke had more to lose than me.

"Hey, Tanner?" Luke asked. I looked at him out of instinct but was puzzled when he wasn't staring at me. He was staring at the grave acting like Tanner was able to talk back. "We all miss you." Luke looked at the candle and in one swish motion he blew it out. He got up and dusted his pants off, holding out his hand. "Let's get something to eat, I'm starving and I'm done being sad."

I reluctantly looked at the grave next to me and looked at the candle in Luke's hand. He pawed it to each hand and I nodded my head. He smiled in return and I grabbed the candle from his grip. I motioned for him to continue forward and I would catch up. When Luke was out of sight and hopefully warming up the car, I quietly took the matchbox that I had in my pocket and struck one up. I winced in pain as I accidentally caught my nail on the flame but was determined to relight the candle that Luke had destroyed. You just don't blow out someone's candle. That's low.

When I saw that Luke disappear ahead, I took one final look at Tanner's grave and knelt to it. I quietly whispered words I have never said and they tasted like venom.

"I love you so much, Tanner." I pecked the dirty grave and half-smiled at the foul taste that was on my lips. "Love, Chloe."

That was the first time I've acknowledged my real name since last year and it felt different. I felt guilty as I shuffled away but I led myself towards Luke's car and plopped onto his uncomfortable seats. Luke hasn't started his car yet and I was a bit curious until he looked at me with a half hint smile on his face. He showed me the keys and thought he was nuts until I realized what he was doing.

"Let's walk around town." I knew what he wanted me to do. He wanted me to see that everybody else has moved on since Tanner has died but I knew that wasn't true. His mom, his best friend, and his girlfriend were the only ones that would never get over it.

I wrapped my arms around myself and walked along with Luke in complete silence. I stared up at the sky and noticed how it wasn't that cliché moment in movies where it's a sad scene so it's about to rain. Instead, it was the bright sunny scene. It was a bit chilly but you wouldn't be able to tell if this were a movie. If this were a movie, it would look like a peaceful scene in which something good was about to happen. In reality, it was a depressing mood where the sun threatened to burn you alive.

As we neared the center of town, I couldn't stop myself from wondering if anyone would recognize me. The last time I was here was two years ago and I've changed so much since then. I've lost weight, I don't have glasses, and I don't straighten my hair anymore, I just let it in the natural curls that look good on me. I know that everyone else must've changed but I never kept in contact with any of them because I was never friends with any of them.

As for Summer, I just pictured her to be taller and maybe chunkier. I pictured her as still having her blonde hair and baby blue eyes. She must've gotten more of a backbone and I could mentally picture her wearing skinny jeans and a tank top with a vest over the top because that would be her style now. But I wasn't sure because the last time I talked to Summer face-to-face was before Tanner's death. I never talked to her afterward because I stopped going to school. My world just felt like it was crashing down even though I didn't let it affect me when random people started texting me and saying that they were sorry for my loss because I buried my emotions.

"There are more people than last time," Luke noted. Snapping out of my thoughts, I looked around to see that we were on the outskirts and that cars were parked all with the little shops everywhere. There was even an apartment building near and there was now a stoplight in the middle of the four-way. It used to be just a stop sign area.

As we roamed closer, I could see the line of random houses on the street and looked to see our house. I was a little curious to see who was living there now, but I knew that you couldn't kick people out of any house.

AMY KULP

They've been living there for two years; I couldn't possibly kick them out now. They were probably a decent part of the community and were well-liked.

Most people from this area are.

"Come on," Luke said. I looked down at the pavement again and followed him faster than before. I didn't even object when he stopped in front of a familiar restaurant and opened the door for me to follow. He knew that I didn't like this food but I was going to deal with it now because I wanted to only have good memories in this town.

I followed him in the back and waited for a server to come for us after we were done. In the meantime, I sat down and looked at how the décor changed. The last time I was here was the first time I was here. I had a really bad time because the owners were naturally noisy and all of the waiters were friendly and bubbly but there was one who was extremely loud and didn't know how to whisper. It drove me crazy. If I judged them just on their food, I would come back because the pasta bowl—which is what I had the first time I came—was amazing. It sent my taste buds on a ride and I have yet to have any other restaurant be able to replicate what I had that first time. It was a five-star meal.

"How can I serve you all?" I looked up to see a beautiful girl with shampoo bottle-blonde hair and looked over to my brother to see his reaction. He stared intently at the menu indicating he knew who that was and hoped she didn't recognize him. I was a little too interested in his story because I didn't even realize he ordered for me until she was gone and hopping around to serve other tables. We sat in silence until I looked around to see if she was in the room anymore. I was going to know the story whether I had to figure it out from him or her.

"Explain?" I pressured.

Luke huffed at me but didn't open his mouth to respond. When she came back, she lightly sat our drinks on the table and smiled as she walked away. I wasn't too sure if she was just naturally friendly or if she was just overworking it because my brother was not terrible looking.

"She's one of my classmates," he whispered. He shrugged his shoulders and popped his straw out. He blew on it a bit and it came flying towards me but I didn't even yell at him this time. I knew there was something more to it than that but I honestly didn't want to know if Luke didn't even want to tell me. "She's gotten prettier over the years."

I felt the skin on my nose pinch together and I felt my eyebrows drop down my face and crease together. She must've had an emotional toll on him because he was never speechless when it came to girls. Usually, he would tell me something disgusting and how he ditched her afterward, and then I would secretly hope that we weren't blood-related because I felt for the girls. We sat in silence though. I didn't want to pressure him to talk about her. As nosey as I was, I could try to respect this boundary.

"Here's your food," the waitress said with a smile on her face. I sniffed the air and looked at what I had gotten on my food and gave Luke a face when I noticed it was a salad with a crispy bowl on the outside. I always loved these types of things and I'm glad that Luke remembered. She gave us napkins and utensils and left with a smile on her face. I glanced back at her and noticed that as she was talking to another employee, she kept darting her eyes towards us. I was wondering if we looked familiar in any way to her and I guiltily wished that she wouldn't remember him.

I quietly took a piece of my outer shell for my food and bit the end off. I ate in silence knowing that Luke was either thinking too hard about everything or he was too busy savoring the taste of the family-owned restaurant. Everyone went here and it was even featured on a couple of TV shows.

Great publicity.

Luke silently rose his hand—gesturing that he wanted the waitress again. She came bouncing over with the checkbook but stood there for a moment too long. I knew she wanted something but I wasn't sure if Luke saw. He was too busy looking at how much it had cost.

"Yes?" I questioned. Her smile faltered a bit but my speaking was enough to get Luke's interest. She turned to him and the feared words came out of her mouth.

"I'm sorry but you look familiar. Do I know you?" Luke looked over at me and arched his eyebrow. I silently nodded yes and listened to him explain how he knew her. The smile on her face didn't fade and I eventually found myself leaving the table. Before I exited the restaurant, I looked back to see that she was now sitting in my seat and they were happily chatting away.

Chatting like old acquaintances.

Stepping out onto the streets, I couldn't help but let my mind drift off to Summer. After all this time, with very few calls between us, I was finally wondering how she was and what she looked like now. I semi wondered if she still lived in the same place as she did before. Letting my curiosity get the better of me, I started walking towards her old home. As I neared her place, I finally realized where I was and I slowed down immensely. I turned my head around a couple of times and looked at my messages to distract me.

Luke didn't even ask where I was. Therefore, I knew he was still busy with that girl in the restaurant and I couldn't help but feel a little jealous. I know that I'm a very awkward person and that I didn't completely trust Luke—any male at all—but that didn't mean he didn't have to worry about me. I secretly wanted someone to try and break me and figure out what happened to me, why I turned out the way I am.

Getting enough courage to go through with it, I walked up the lovely stepping stones and opened the screen door to Summer's house. I breathed in and out in one motion and knocked on the door. I heard about two big dogs barking and a small one yipping at me. I smiled a bit and hoped that Summer lived here. If this was still her house, those dogs would recognize me in an instant.

As the door opened, I began to step back so that whoever answered the door would know it was me. I know I've changed but for the most part, I'm still me.

"Hello?"

"Uh, hi," I said uncomfortably. "Is Summer here?" I stood silent for a moment while their eyes looked me up and down and I felt a bit impatient. "Is she here?"

"Uh." Summer's mom stood uncertain for a minute and she kept glancing at me like she knew who I was. "Who are you?" Ouch, that hurt.

"I'm, uh, C-Chloe," I questioned, wondering if she remembered me. Nothing rang a bell in her face. "Summer's friend and Tanner's old girlfriend?" I wondered. Something must've clicked because she snapped her fingers and brought me into an instant hug.

When we retracted, she looked behind her and frowned. "I think Summer's at the cemetery." I nodded my head and waited to leave but she kept talking. "You've changed, you know." I nodded my head and I guess she knew I only came for her daughter because she nodded her head and went back inside.

Even though I was now athletic, I huffed at the idea and began my trench to the graveyard. It was going to be a while and I knew that if Luke was still talking to his friend I would have to tell him where I was going. No way would I allow myself to go without telling him because, at the cemetery, you don't get bars.

As I looked at the sky, it seemed that the sun would be setting soon. I know that I didn't tell my parents that we would be a state away and I'm sure Luke didn't, so I knew that I needed to make this quick. We would have to arrive home before our parents. I'm not sure if they would like the idea that we're a state away without them and we didn't bring overloads of food and water. They always loved being prepared in case of natural disasters and we would get in trouble if we didn't bring them. Not that we didn't ask them. That we didn't bring them.

Looking around the graveyard, I could've sworn the sky had gotten darker as I approached. It felt very ominous, but I knew I had to keep my hopes up high. I was going to see Summer for the first time since I had left. Like in a horror movie where the girl gets herself in an obvious situation and the scary music starts to play. I shook the thought from my head and headed towards Tanner's grave anyway.

"Hey, get away from his grave!" I yelled. I ran over and pushed the person away from my boyfriend's grave. I was insulted that this person would even think about disgracing someone else's grave like that. She had a candle in hand and I didn't want to wait to see what she would've done with it. "What's the matter with you?" I asked-yelled. My stance stayed the same and I felt my chin turn hard, waiting for a reply to my answer.

As the girl turned to face me, I looked at the delicate fingers holding the candle and saw that it was the same candle as last time. I looked back at the grave and noticed that she was holding the same one. In its place, a dozen roses were lying still and on the dirt path. I looked back to the girl and noticed tears falling down her porcelain cheeks.

"Chloe?" I blinked for a moment and stared at the girl on the ground. She clutched the candle harder to herself and she turned herself around so she was sitting with her legs crossed over each other. I looked deeper at her and took notice of what she was wearing.

This girl has pitch black hair that was dyed. In the hair were blonde and pink highlights and she had bangs. Her clothes were all dull and black with a pair of converse at the side. I looked closer at her face and noticed the way her dimples lay on her cheeks. She was trying hard not to cry as she looked at me.

My insides deteriorated.

"S-Summer?" The face of my old best friend began blubbering and she dropped the unscented candle on the ground and leaned in to hug me. I hugged her back with a confused face. This wasn't the best friend I left behind.

My Summer, the real Summer, was the chubby girl with tanned skin and a happy attitude. She had blonde hair with a childlike atmosphere that everyone couldn't help but love. This girl was like a voodoo doll with death smeared all around her.

Maybe I was just stereotyping.

Once she let go of me, she wiped the tears from her face and sat down. I kneeled beside her—a little numb—and we sat in silence for a couple of minutes.

"I-I'm sorry about pushing you," I whispered. I could feel movement beside me and I could tell that Summer was listening."I was just expecting the real you."

Truthfully, I felt foolish. I have never been a violent person, but twice in one week, I had managed to hurt two different, innocent people. I knew never to use violence on anyone, whether it was accidental or not. I was punished because of Aaron. I needed to keep my emotions locked in my head because now I had hurt Summer. She wasn't just some delinquent trying to mess with someone's grave, she was here to heal herself. I probably took that safe place away from her.

"The real me?" Summer complained. "This is the real me. With what I've been through, I deserve to be like this. My best friend died and then the other left me without saying goodbye." I bit my inner cheek and let her continue to talk about me. "I don't have any friends and I don't want to be known as the child girl anymore. I wanted to be me. Summer. The real me."

"You don't..." I paused and let out a breath. "You don't do drugs or anything do you?"

"That's just rude, Chloe," Summer asked. I felt a guilty pang in my body. "I could guess so much about you if you would like." She turned to face me and I did the same. She grabbed an article of clothing on my body and looked at it as trash. "You would never wear this. The

AMY KULP

geek you would never wear this." Ouch. "I loved your straight hair and your wire-framed glasses." My hand flew up to my nose and mentally pushed the glasses up my face. "I liked the skinny you, not the muscular you." She wrapped her hand around my bicep and squeezed. "The new you scares me. But we have to move on because this is a one-day thing. You'll most likely not talk to me after this like you've been doing for two years." Summer sighed and looked back at Tanner's grave. "I hated you for so long." I wrapped my arms around my legs. "I blamed you for Tanner dying and I have no idea why." I agree with her on this one, though. I blamed myself so much for Tanner's death and a little piece of me still does.

Maybe if I was a little more attached to Tanner, he would've graciously gotten home faster and would've never met the drunken driver. Maybe if I had gone with him as he asked, I would be the one dead—not him. But that would put him through so much and I don't want him to suffer as I have. His dad and he were coming to pick me up. If I had agreed to get driven to their house, they would never have died. They were coming for me. They didn't deserve to die. It was all my fault.

"Chloe?"

I began uncontrollably shaking without feeling and I kept thinking about how Tanner dying was my fault. Then it slowly progressed into more memories that I don't want to remember. It reminded me not to trust anyone and especially no males.

I began stressing myself out.

"Chloe? What's going on?"

I felt my back hit the ground and I began shaking uncontrollably. I thought more and more into it and I couldn't help but close my eyes. I whispered the only things that could come out of my mouth before I unwillingly passed out.

"My fault."

Chapter Eight

When I got home, I couldn't help but feel betrayed as I walked through the house to find Luke. He was making out with a random girl on the couch. As I stood there watching them, I noticed it wasn't the girl he was with during school. I scoffed at the idea of him and stomped my way upstairs. I couldn't believe he chose his girlfriend over me. Again. Even worse was that she probably wasn't his girlfriend. She was just some girl who threw her body at him. I slammed my door shut very loud and hoped that it scared both of them out of the liplock. Our mom and dad weren't home so they probably thought they could have their privacy. I'm always upstairs anyway.

   I threw my backpack on the floor and felt my body begin to crumble to the floor. I kneeled before I could recount what just happened and touched my neck with an easy touch. With an I-might-break-this touch. It felt painful and I slowly rolled both of my hands over my neck until it reached my shoulders. I made myself relax for a moment and then got off the ground and made myself go towards the dressers that had a mirror. I grabbed a pair of sweatpants and an old T and undressed. Stopping at the sight of me, I looked at the hickey on my neck and looked at the rest of my body.

   Nobody thinks you're pretty.

I looked at my reflection once again and took a good look at myself. I did have a pimple on my chin and I did have quite a nose. Kind of crooked unless I turned my head to a certain angle. Looking at the rest of my body, I noted that my shoulders were too square for my frame, my fingers were too bony, and I wasn't skinny. I wasn't fat, but I wasn't skinny. I was midsized.

Skinny girls are always pretty.

Tapping my fingers against my dresser, I bit my lip for a moment and then put my clothes on. I quickly grabbed my sneakers and shoved them onto my feet. Looking for my music player, I grabbed a pair of headphones and made my way down the stairs. I would have to worry about the hickey some other time. I was on a mission right now.

I was disgusted to see that Luke and the girl were still hanging all over each other. It's like they didn't even hear me slam the door upstairs. Or maybe they didn't care. Either way, I quickly made my way to the kitchen.

What did I need to jog? I searched through the fridge before deciding on grabbing some water. Did you need a snack for a jog? I have never exercised before so I wasn't sure what was normal. I'm assuming that since my goal was to lower my body weight I shouldn't pack a snack. Right? I was a little hungry though. Maybe I should eat before I start jogging. I grabbed a banana from the tabletop and started thinking about my mom. She always wanted a jogging partner but I always denied her offers. She would be thrilled if I told her that I wanted to start.

I quickly texted her and told her that I was now going to start working out. When she finally replied, I half-smiled but put the phone away. I took a bite from the banana and threw the peel away as I downed the rest of it. I was going to eat healthily as my mother suggested and I would hopefully take up a sport. Sports keep people in shape. Especially now that I was in an upper grade. I know that they practiced almost every day and on days where they didn't, they would work out together. I knew that I would need to start slow though. If I change everything about myself too quickly, it often ends up with me quitting.

Placing the earphones in place and turning my volume up, I began to slowly walk down the street. It was a bit chilly out but I could easily deal with this since I would begin to sweat at any minute.

The jog got my mind off the topic and that was the best thing for me at the moment. I needed the distraction.

***

"Please," Summer whispered in my ear. I slowly opened my eyes and looked up at the sky. When my eyes adjusted from the darkness, I looked towards Summer and saw that she seemed to be upset and was looking at the gravestone of Tanner and me. "Thank god." She tugged at the ends of her dark sweater and pulled until they were covering her fingers and she could squeeze them closed. "You were out for an hour, I'm surprised your brother didn't come searching for you."

"An hour?"

"No," Summer finally said. "More like ten minutes but it felt like an hour. Are you okay?" she asked. She didn't seem much worried about me but enough to let any surrounding people know that she didn't do it and that she was worried for her ex-friend.

"I'm fine," I whispered. I don't even know why I fainted. That was my first time fainting ever, I naturally don't faint. Maybe I was under a lot of stress when I did it or maybe I just did it so she would stop blaming me but I don't want to know why I fainted. I could remember everything beforehand perfectly fine but the moment you ask me for the exact reason for the fainting is the moment I will stop talking to you.

"How long are you planning on staying here?" Summer questioned.

"Until Luke's ready to go but before my parents get home." I shrugged my shoulders as I looked towards the cemetery clock. Luke must have not been concerned about our parents finding out where we were because they were already home. Although I'm certain that they didn't know we were here. They probably texted both of us, but I wouldn't be able to receive it while I was here. I wonder if he would tell them where we were.

"Where is Luke?"

"Talking to an old friend," I replied. I didn't enjoy talking about Luke to Summer though. I knew that she had a massive crush and might still have one, but I didn't want to talk about my brother. I wanted to talk about her. Or me. Or us.

We sat in silence for a while and we just stared at Tanner's grave. Once in a while, I would catch her staring at me and I would look her way, for her to quickly look back at the gravestone. I wouldn't mind too much since I was also staring at her and from time to time she would catch me too. As the weather got colder, I could see the goosebumps rising on her arms but she would rub her arms and they would disappear for the next instant.

"Can I ask you a question?" she finally asked. I slowly nodded my head without hesitation because I knew that she wanted to ask the question the whole time. Even though I was gone for two years, I still knew my best friend's personality and behavioral patterns. "Why didn't you ever call me back?"

That's the question I've been pondering for ages.

"I don't know," I truthfully answered. Summer searched my face for the truth and once she realized I was telling it, she placed her hands in her face. "I've been trying to figure it out for a while now but I don't know why I've never called you for the first year."

As Summer lifted her head out of her hands, I could tell that she caught the loophole in my sentence. She looked at me with pleading eyes and hoped that I would tell her about the second year but we both secretly knew I would never tell a soul. I was good at keeping secrets, but it felt natural to tell her everything.

"I guess it's because every year I move, I always want to forget what life was like the year before." I sighed and looked at my breath as it got caught in the frigid air. "I never forget but I wanted to forget about my boyfriend and his family. I wanted to forget about sarcastic Dorothy Of Oz," I whispered. I smiled at Summer but she grimaced at the name. "I didn't want to see you hurting because I've always seen you hurt. Now that you didn't have another friend to stick up for you, I didn't want to be the only one. I knew that you called Tanner at night because you started to believe what bullies said. After all, he told me later." I looked at the grave quietly. "And I always wanted to comfort you too but I didn't want to see you upset. I didn't want to be the one to tell you everything was alright because we both knew that was a lie."

"A lot has changed since Tanner died." That was all she said before I heard the familiar voice of my brother. She looked at the distance and smiled dully at me. "Don't try to call me now, Chloe."

I wanted to protest with her that I would call her but my voice didn't come out and my body began walking towards the path towards Luke's car. I wanted to say goodbye to her but I knew that it was just a wasted breath. I knew how stubborn she was. She held grudges. I didn't blame her though. I would dislike her if the roles were reversed. She would remember this day but she would never forgive me for leaving her.

She would never forgive me for being selfish.

Making my way down the dulled path of graves, I felt bad for the headstones that were barely visited that had dust or were beat up. Remembering how Tanner's grave was, I could tell that Summer had to visit often. His stone was clean and the area around it was pristine. She probably told Tanner all of her problems.

Like the olden days.

I'm sure his mom visited too. I couldn't bring myself to see her though. I haven't seen her since before his death. I never sent my condolences and now I felt like it was too late. She probably felt abandoned too. She lost her husband and her son. That must have been devastating to her.

Seeing the car we came in, I slowed my pace down and noticed how dark the sky was. It was pitch dark out now. I suddenly felt colder as I entered the car and saw the happy glow on my brother's face. It was clear that his conversation with the waitress had gone over well. He reconnected with someone and I was once again jealous. Although I reconnected with Summer, it wasn't the same interaction. It gave me a bigger pit in my stomach.

"How was seeing Tanner again?" he asked obliviously. I shrugged my shoulders at Luke and he just nodded his head. He was in too good of a mood to notice anything off about me. Then again, I'm not even sure if he knew naturally when something was off about me.

Besides the obvious crying.

Our car ride home was very quiet and I could tell that Luke was getting tired. He made the car extra cold so that he wouldn't fall asleep on the way there and he wouldn't let me turn the radio on to slow music for my sleeping habits. I attempted to fall asleep once but the road began getting bumpy when we were near our house.

"Almost there," he whispered to me. My body froze in place but it didn't make a difference since it was like that for almost two hours. He drummed his fingers against the steering wheel until we made it home and when he parked, he bolted out. For someone who was extremely tired, I expected him to move at a slower speed.

I got out slowly though because I knew that my foot and leg had fallen asleep together. Plus I was tired and I didn't want to get out of the comfortable spot that I was in. Knowing that our parents would be in the doorway ready to lecture us, I took my time extra slow and when I was on the porch, I listened for any yelling.

It was dead silent so I knew that they were waiting for me.

As I crept in the front door, instead of running towards my room like I was intending, I went towards the living room. Luke was sitting on the couch reading a note with his lips silently reading. I sat down next to him and read what he was reading.

I stared at the paper for a bit too long since it only consisted of a warning that we were grounded when they came home and reread it ten times before Luke decided to speak.

"This is why I don't do things for you," he whispered. He slammed the paper on the coffee table and looked at me with fury in his eyes. "I always get in trouble when I do things for you!" he shouted. I winced at his volume and he pushed past me and ran up the stairs.

I stayed frozen in place until I heard his door slam shut and then I sat down on the couch. I hated that he blamed me for how our parents would react to this. He knew what he was signing up for and that he might get in trouble. I covered myself with the blankets on the couch to make myself feel warm and fuzzy. I stared off into the darkness instead of going up the stairs.

"But you owe me," I finally whispered as I drifted off into sleep.

Chapter Nine

"Mom?" I came up towards her casually and she raised her eyebrows in interest. She swallowed the rest of the cream cheese bagel in her mouth and wiped it before paying any attention to me. Before I could get anything out, she smiled at me and hugged me. I wasn't sure why until she started speaking.

"I'm so glad you want to get healthy with me. It's so much harder to do it by yourself," she said. "How about we go jogging tonight around four?"

"Sure," I said, nodding my head. She ruffled my hair and smiled sweetly at me. Trying to get ready for work, she grabbed her coffee and sniffed it before drinking it. I wanted to talk to her but she always seemed too busy. She was always on the move.

"Make sure to eat kiddo," she said. I turned towards the pantry and grabbed a box of corn flakes. She smiled once more at me before she put her jacket on and started to walk towards her car.

"Mom?" I asked-yelled. She turned towards me impatiently and I licked my lips. "Can I stay home from school today?" Panic automatically struck her face.

"Why? Are you sick?" She retraced her steps to put the back of her hand to my forehead. "You don't have a fever." She quickly pulled a jar of Advil from her purse and handed it to me. "You probably just have cramps.

Take two of these every four hours and you'll be fine."
Before I could get another word out, she kissed my
forehead and took off out the door.

Staring down at my hand, I rolled my eyes and
placed the pill bottle on the coffee table. I felt myself tear
up as she dismissed me completely. I guess I had to get
ready since I had to go to school. If Luke asked I'm pretty
sure mom would keep his side for sure. Since it was me, I
was only sick because I had cramps. I wasn't even sick
though. I just didn't want to go to school. If she wanted to
assume it was because I was sick, I would let her think
that. I put my cornflakes back on the shelf and sighed.

I made my way up to my room and closed my
bedroom door behind me. I got some of my clothes out
and stared in the mirror for ten minutes. I stared at the
hickeys on my neck and stared at my body. Every time I
looked in the mirror, I could see more imperfections that I
hadn't seen before. Once I realized that I was
procrastinating, I lifted my shirt off and stared at my
stomach for a couple of minutes. Frowning, I quickly put
my other shirt on and didn't dare look at my thighs as I
put my jeans on. I could just see how big they both were
without having to see the skin to prove it to myself.

As quick as I could, I put my hair in a ballerina
bun and gasped to see my neck. I knew that I had the
hickeys, but they seemed more noticeable than yesterday.
Looking for my makeup, I reached for the bottle when I
stopped myself.

Your mother doesn't think you're pretty, why else would she buy you makeup?

I shook my head at myself. I wasn't using this for my face, I was using it to cover up my demon marks. Sighing, I dipped my finger in my liquid foundation and turned my head to the right angle. Silently applying them to the marks, I wasn't paying attention to the footsteps outside of my bedroom door so I didn't have time to react when my door was flung open.

*"Are those **hickeys**?"*

***

I wasn't fully prepared to go back to boxing today. I skipped two days of it on probation and the one day I worked, I barely worked out afterward. I have also been eating my soul out without thinking about the intake. I've been out of control with my emotions. I haven't even exercised it off by running. I was so sluggish because of it that I knew I would have my ass handed to me today. I had to think about the commitment I had made though. One of the few promises Missy made everyone keep was that we had to attend at least once a week. There were circumstances that she would allow for this to be broken, but not wanting to go is not a reason. If we didn't go for a week, we were never allowed back in her gym again. We didn't even get a refund for it.

I threw my bag on the locker room floor and grabbed a water bottle that was placed in there. I carried it with me while I took out my tape to prepare my blisters. I knew that since I haven't been working out, my blisters were open back up and would hurt worse. I would probably have more too.

"Tanner!" Missy yelled. I huffed at the sound of my name. I understand that this is a small gym so that we get personal attention, but I wanted to train without being interrupted. Couldn't I have one day to myself? I turned around from where I was and waited for her to walk over to me. She took her time and when she finally got to me, she just stared. Before she spoke, I knew that I wouldn't like what she had to say to me. "We have a new company policy. I want you to know that there was a lot of thought put into this. For the safety of everyone, we are implementing a rule about no jewelry." She looked at the necklace around my neck and held her hand out.

I wasn't going to give this to her. I was okay with putting it in my gym bag but I wasn't about to cough it up. My eyebrows furrowed at her thought process but I unhooked it regardless. Without letting me explain that I was going to put it in my bag, she took it off of me. I wasn't sure where she was going but she walked away from me. I stood there for a second before looking around. Did that actually happen or was I daydreaming about it?

I finally caught someone's eyes and I felt myself walking towards them. They saw what had just gone down and he was looking a little guilty. As I approached, he turned back to the bag he was at and I felt myself tapping him on the shoulder. He pretended to act surprised that I was there but I knew that it was fake. We made direct eye contact before I came over.

"Was it because of me pushing you to the ground?" I asked. For a second, he acted like he didn't know what I was talking about. I didn't like that he was trying to play dumb but he eventually caught on. He nodded his head slightly and I saw a pink blush creep along his cheeks. "Do you believe me when I say that it was accidental?" He hesitated and bit his lip as he thought about it. That small body gesture made me aware that he wasn't sure if he believed me. I nodded my head and knew not to blame him. If I saw someone beating up someone else, I would say something too. Here, Aaron had that power over me. "Do you know where she took it?"

"No idea." He shrugged his shoulders and looked at me. "Maybe ask her once you leave? She can't keep it."

"That's what I thought," I whispered. I nodded my head and took the bag next to him. I just wanted to make sure that I wasn't going crazy. Besides, I don't think Missy would overreact to the point where she would take my personal property. She wasn't that kind of person.

Everything about Missy screamed anti-bullying. She advertised her gym as a bully-free zone and when bringing in new members, often emphasized that boxing is for defensive purposes, never for fighting. It was drilled into my head when I first joined as well. I speculated that is why she picked Aaron to be her scholarship boxer this year. He was bullied and wanted to be able to protect himself. It fit her brand so well.

I couldn't help but let my anger come through me though. It wasn't necessarily just about her taking the necklace. It was about everything in my life. I hit the punching bag harder than I ever felt I had before. I winced in pain from the skin breaking, but I kept putting more power into the punches. Every ounce of sweat was worth it. Every blister was worth it. As I continued to punch, I realized that my anger wasn't towards Aaron or Missy. It wasn't towards Luke or Summer.

It was towards *him*.

I felt my punches becoming weaker as my mind unwillingly flashed back to memories that shouldn't have to be remembered. I felt my body beginning to slow down to the point where I felt like a snail. I ate breakfast this morning so I knew that my blood sugar wasn't low. It wasn't my body doing this to me though. It was my mind that was protecting itself.

My mind was playing tricks on me because for a minute I didn't even want to fight. I just wanted to cry. This was a place where I could let out all of my anger. Why did I want to cry? I wouldn't let myself cry again. I have been crying way too much this past month. The strong exterior of me didn't let me cry. Instead, I placed sloppy punches into the bag. I couldn't feel the pain in my hands anymore. I must have looked like a hot mess because I soon felt a hand on my shoulder. I stopped punching the bag and turned towards the reassuring hand.

"Are you okay, Tanner?" Aaron asked. I breathed out from holding my breath and took his hand off of my shoulder. My shoulders were slumped and my posture was no longer straight. I'm sure that this was the first sign to Aaron that I was not okay. I forced myself to have perfect posture. When I went through the phase where I wanted to lose weight, I read somewhere that if you had good posture, it helped burn more calories that way. That has always stuck with me even though I'm not sure if it's true or false. "I'll go get your necklace," Aaron whispered to me. He immediately ran off but I stayed where I was. I didn't need the necklace right now but I didn't want him to know that. He was just trying to help me. When he came back, he handed it to me and looked behind him. "I'm sorry about the necklace." I focused on taking my deep breaths to calm myself down. "Missy's just upset that you have been skipping out on us." I had no idea what he was talking about. I opened one of my eyes and looked at him with a confused expression. When he saw me looking, he further explained it to me. "Yesterday was the big tournament sign-ups." I shrugged my shoulders and turned to see what he was doing with my necklace.

"I wouldn't have been able to go anyways," I mumbled without stuttering.

"Why not?" Aaron asked. He was fiddling with my necklace to try and get the pendant back onto the chain.

"Missy only pays for one of our spots and that was you. I wouldn't have been able to pay for it." I shrugged my shoulders again and walked towards my bench for water.

"Aren't you rich?" Aaron asked. I nodded my head but didn't feel like further explaining it to him.

My family didn't just give me the money. I worked for it and if I couldn't work for it, I had to give reasoning why I should be able to do this. Both my mom and dad were very against me joining boxing. We all agreed that as long as I did it for protection and didn't do it as a sport, they would pay for it. If I wanted to join it as a sport, I would have to pay for my tournaments and rides. It was too much of a hassle for me to want to do it as a sport. Missy knew about it but I hadn't told anybody else. She should have remembered that.

When Aaron was done fixing the necklace, he looked proud of himself. He walked around me and I felt my shoulders tense up. "I'm sure she would've struck a deal with you," he mumbled. "Let me put this on you." As he flung the chain and pendant around my neck, I froze.

***

"Chloe, I have your necklace," the science teacher told me. I turned around confused since I have never parted with my necklace. I stared intently when I saw him holding it out for me to see. I touched my neck to make sure it wasn't an imposter and was horrified to note that that was mine. I just wasn't sure how he had gotten it.

I had avoided answering any questions or giving him any eye contact at all during this whole period. I was positive that I was wearing it before I had gotten in the room but I wasn't exactly sure how he had gotten it. It was truly a mystery because I would've known if it had fallen off in the middle of class. I would have also heard it if it fell on the desk or the floor. How did he get my necklace?

I didn't wait for everyone to leave the room before I started walking towards him. He wouldn't do anything if there were witnesses. I reached my hand out in front of me and tried to clasp onto the pendant. At the last possible second, he pulled it from my grasp and smiled creepily at me. I instantly looked around the room to see if anyone could witness it but was horrified to see that no one was in here. Where was his next class? Shouldn't they be filing in here soon?

"Let me put it on." I furrowed my eyebrows and nodded no. I knew what he would do and I didn't want a repeat of yesterday. "You won't get it back unless…" He dangled it in from my face as if it was a warning and I couldn't help but bite my lip.

I couldn't live without that necklace. It was the only thing that I had left of Tanner and I needed something to calm me down during the day. I needed it but I wasn't sure what lengths I would go to to get it. He couldn't possibly do anything during the school day. Right?

"You have a split second choice," he mumbled. He started putting it in his pocket and I knew that he wasn't *joking around. Although I could tell my parents about him stealing it, there wasn't any proof that he had. There were no cameras in the school so everything he did was him versus me.*

Gaining tears in my eyes, I walked closer to him and felt my breath catch in my throat. I slowly turned around for him and didn't breathe as he placed the necklace slowly around my neck. I jumped half a mile when he touched his fingers to my neck but then I realized he was just moving my hair to the side. Deciding that I didn't want him to touch me, I grabbed most of it and held onto it as I placed it on the side of my neck.

As soon as I heard the click of the necklace, I rushed out of the room. I knew that the bell had rung but I didn't care. My breath was shallow and my heart was racing. I slowly inched my hair the way it originally was and covered any marks on my neck.

As I walked to my next class, I couldn't help but look back at the room I had just left. He didn't try anything this time. He didn't even hint that he wanted to do anything to me. He didn't even hint about the other night. Maybe he realized that what he did was wrong. Maybe he just wanted to start all over.

Maybe him returning my necklace was an apology.

***

"Stop!" I whimpered. I turned around and swatted the necklace out of Aaron's hand. As soon as it hit the ground, I picked it up and bolted to the changing room. I felt like I was going to cry but thankfully I handled myself pretty decently. Tears were not gathering in the corner of my eyes and I didn't feel my lip quiver from the possibility of crying. Seeing as there was no one in the bathroom with me, I went over by the trash. "You have caused me so much pain." I kissed my pendant and placed it in the trash. "I love you Tanner but..." I shook my head at the thought and grabbed my gym bag.

Walking out of the changing room, I was relieved that I didn't see Aaron. I walked towards the front desk and smiled at the receptionist. She was friendly but I didn't know her.

"Can you tell Missy I'm leaving early?"

"For what?" she asked. I was puzzled and I could tell she knew that I was thinking of a very good excuse. "How about I put that it's a family emergency?" she questioned. I nodded my head and thanked her as I walked out of the gym with my gym bag on my shoulder.

Since I wasn't supposed to be out of the gym yet, I was forced to walk home. It wasn't that bad since I needed the exercise and it wasn't that far of a walk—maybe twenty minutes long. The only bad part about the walk was that I had time to think. I attempted to keep my mind occupied with street signs and cars that passed by but I failed miserably.

As I got to my house, I was interested in why my mom was home so early. It was only four and she usually didn't come home until six. Walking closer to the house, I couldn't help but feel a bit worried about what I could walk into. Every time mom came home early it was because we had to move or very terrible news was to come. I've noticed lately that she hasn't been at work too much. She was either going in later, coming home earlier or not showing up at all.

I screeched the door open and quietly closed it. I walked towards the kitchen since that's where the light was on and I was surprised to see her in her jogging outfit. She stopped exercising with me for a while and it kind of hurt that she did it secretly.

"Oh, hey, Chloe. What are you doing home so early?" She looked like a toddler that got caught with his hand in the cookie jar.

"I... uh..." I didn't exactly know what to say since I wasn't expecting to have to explain to anyone why I was home. "Why are you home so early?"

"I'm taking a little break from work today," she said smiling. "Want to go for a jog? You weren't supposed to come out of the gym for another hour so I don't suspect that you did much yet."

"Yeah, sure." I nodded my head and dropped my gym bag as she got her running shoes on. Grabbing the water from my bag, I headed out the door and started jogging without her. I wanted to know why she was home so early because I knew that she was lying. I wasn't going to complain about spending time with her though. It wasn't often that we had this time together.

"You have to wait up, I'm old," she said, already out of breath. I slowed my pace a little and I think she gave me a devil face because when she started walking beside me, she didn't speak at all. "So are you going to tell me why you're home so early from boxing? The thing we pay for?"

"Um, she ended classes early for family emergencies," I whispered. I was hoping that she would drop the topic but knowing my mom, she wanted to know every detail.

"What happened?"

"Her, uh, toddler got sick," I whispered even softer.

"She's too young to have a child, she's about four years older than you." She's five years older than me but I'm not hinting anything to my mom. Besides, my mom is one to talk to. She had Luke at age eighteen with my dad. "Anyway, if you keep missing out on those boxing lessons, I don't see the reason for you to go to them anymore."

"Mom!" I stopped in my tracks and stared at her as she continued walking. She didn't even turn around when she noticed I left her, she kept going. I headed back to my room and wondered quietly why she was acting the way she was. She never threatened my boxing before. All of a sudden she comes home early and decides to be a parent?

Is it possible that she had lost her job? It explained why she was always home now. It explained why she got so mad about the possible money I was wasting. My mom couldn't lose her job though. Could she?

I tried not to let her bother me though. I just sat in my room for a bit. I needed someone to talk to and I know that I didn't have anyone's number except for Summer and Tanner's. Summer warned me not to call her so the only other choice was Tanner.

"Hey, Tanner, I, uh…" I thought for a moment. "I miss you bunches but I think when I went to your grave I had the realization that you aren't… coming back. I'm sorry and I'll always love you but…" I shook my head and turned my phone off.

That was much harder than I thought it'd be.

Chapter Ten

"Can I speak with you after class?" I nodded my head and smiled as my science teacher went back to his desk. Other students started filing into the room so I got out my supplies to pay attention and take good notes. I admit, after the incident happened a couple of months ago, I was worried about even stepping foot in his room again. He's proven to me that he's changed by not making any advancements towards me that would make me uncomfortable. He had his head screwed on straight and understood that what he did was wrong. Sure, he didn't apologize verbally but I have a hint that's what he wanted to talk about today. Plus I still did his extra credit for him after school without any problems either.

When the class period ended, I packed up slowly and waited until the door closed to sit back down. Nobody was technically allowed to know about the extra credit because of how unfair it would be for them to find out about it. So it wouldn't look suspicious, every day I just made it seem like I just packed up slowly. I also fooled everyone because I made sure to pack up slowly in every other class I had throughout the day as well.

"So you know the test you took yesterday?" I wearily nodded my head and hoped that I would finally get some good news about it. I've been studying more than I ever have for other classes. I wanted to stop doing these extra credit opportunities with him and I figured the only way to do that was if I raised my grade. "Well, you failed it." I found it impossible that I would have failed with how much I have been studying. However, I couldn't find a reason for him to want to lie to me about it. "So I'm going to have you retake the test and you'll need to study until then. Maybe it's something in your studying techniques that is wrong."

"I have other classes though," I said. I was appreciative of this opportunity but I couldn't drop other classes in favor of his. He had to know that it was my least favorite subject. He walked to his desk and started writing on an orange pass. He gave it to me and I shook my head and walked out. An orange pass means you can skip that class if the teacher allows it. I was just hoping that I could because my next two teachers were really strict. The next teacher was extremely difficult since I was predictably always late to her class.

As I started walking down the hall, I was stopped. The science teacher ran after me and I refused to back up so he had to catch up to me, I listened and nodded my head.

"Tell them it's an emergency or something. They'd never let you come down **just** for studying."

When I went to my next classes, I begrudgingly asked if they would let me skip. Each teacher said yes after thoughtful consideration. However, I had to do all of the classwork and homework for tomorrow. I agreed to it but wished that one of them would tell me no. I had *boatloads to do so I hoped that studying for his science test, even more, would help me. I needed a better grade.*

"I'm back," I said out of breath. He shook his head and pointed to a desk upfront. I sat in it hastily and ripped open my books to start studying. I was facing the teacher so I could see all of his moves. Even though I was supposed to be studying, I was distracted by him. He still made me nervous and I was always on edge. He hasn't done anything since that day but I had to keep wishing he wouldn't.

From what I could see, all he was doing was putting in everyone's grades. Once in a while, he would look towards me with interest. He always caught me staring and would immediately look at the computer. I couldn't tell if I was more embarrassed or he was. I had to force myself to concentrate on studying so I began making flashcards for myself. After about ten minutes, I heard him get up from his chair.

When he sat down next to me, I jumped from my seat. I turned towards him to see what he was doing but he just smirked as he looked down at my notes. He closed my books and slid the test towards me. He barely let me study for one whole period, never mind two. As I started filling out the name and date, I felt him continue staring at me. I was normally nervous during tests but he was making me distracted. Was I taking too long to answer the question?

Unfortunately, this version of his test was different than the first one I had taken. I was a bit disappointed but should have expected it. I was specifically looking up answers to questions I had remembered from the prior test. When he noticed my frustration, he chuckled a bit to himself. I tried to focus on taking the test but could see him inching the chair closer to me as I answered questions. The closer he got, the more distracted I had become. At this point, I couldn't even read a sentence without thinking about what he was doing.

As I wrote in an answer, he grabbed my hands and took the pencil from them. I watched as he erased the answer and wrote in the right answer. I immediately felt terrible because this was technically cheating, not extra credit.

"Isn't that cheating?" I asked.

"Not if you don't tell anyone," he mumbled. I watched as he filled out most of my science test and I wished that I protested. Once he was done, he got up and I stayed in my seat because I was morally torn. I didn't want to be known as a cheater. "Well, come on." My eyebrows crinkled as I walked towards his desk. He sat me in his seat and then pointed towards my name and grade. My heart dropped as I looked at the score.

70.

I continued to stare at the screen and felt myself internally scream at myself. I shook my head and swiveled his chair to look at him.

"Are there any other extra credit opportunities that I can do today?" I asked. He nodded his head and gave me a stack of papers with grades on him. Without saying a

word, I knew that he wanted me to plug these into the grade book. From the corner of my eye, I could see him sit down and stare at me. He didn't have anything in front of him and he didn't make it discreet.

"I have a problem." He perked up behind me and leaned over. "These answers are marked differently and I couldn't help but wonder which was correct." He shrugged his shoulders and his face hardened. "I know that it's not my job to look at the papers but—"

"So stick with your job," he sternly said. The change in his voice was enough to make me continue. I looked over at some of the other papers and noticed more mistakes. I couldn't help but bite my lip to try and keep this to myself. Was he just picking and choosing people's grades at random? I know that I shouldn't have judged the teacher but I did and I immediately started changing grades. And I was immediately frightened when he pounded his fist against the desk loud and started yelling at me. "God, Chloe! You're disgusting! Why can't you stick with your job? I did not tell you to grade the papers, did I? Some people got marks on their papers because they cheated! I always take points off for that!" he boomed.

I was never good under pressure so I wasn't surprised when I felt my body begin to shake. Especially since I was never yelled at like that before. I turned back to the computer and deleted all of the grades in that row. Without replacing them, I got up from his chair and grabbed my bookbag. I listened to him get up, but I was *determined to beat him to the door. He raced me for it and as I grabbed the handle to turn it, he slammed his body against the door to close it. I tried the handle again but he wasn't going to budge.*

"Where are you going?" he asked angrily.

"I'm leaving," I said, weakly. "You're scaring me."

"Scaring you?" he questioned. He walked towards me and I walked away from him. "I'm scaring you? I could try if you want me to."

"No, I'm good," I whispered.

"What was that, Chloe? Hmm? What did you say? Tell me louder."

"I said—"

"What was that Chloe?"

"I-I—"

"Repeat it, Chloe, come on. Don't be afraid Chloe. You can do it, you're a big girl."

"No." And that's when the second incident happened.

***

As I walked into my third-period class, I blankly walked to my desk and got out my notes as the male teacher started lecturing. I zoned out and I guess that was bad because he immediately picked on me. I groaned to myself and knew that he only did it so I would pay attention. I just didn't understand how to translate poems and passages from a different time. It didn't make sense to me. I had no idea what he was talking about so I looked towards Aaron as my lifesaver but he wasn't looking at me. I sighed quietly and shrugged my shoulders. Unfortunately, this teacher was not giving up on me and wanted me to answer the question. I wasn't even sure what subject I was in so I attempted to look deep in thought.

"Page twenty-two of your textbook." I flipped through it thankful that he had said something and reread it. I shrugged my shoulders once I was done since I didn't understand it and he placed the chalk down on the blackboard. He shook his head at me and pointed to Aaron who answered the question perfectly and instantly. I felt embarrassed and humiliated that he would call on me. He knows my grades are lower. He had to of known that I wouldn't get the correct answer - it's why my hand wasn't raised. If I had it raised, that means I know the answer.

I looked over at Aaron in disbelief and he stared back at me. Neither of us was breaking eye contact and then I mouthed thanks to him. He shrugged his shoulders and turned back but not before he caught me smiling. I turned back too and attempted to pay attention without much luck. I could not understand what we were talking about and it felt like I was learning a different language. I wanted to cry. Why couldn't I understand this? I have never been this bad at English. I was a low A average.

When the bell rang, I packed up my books and jumped when a hand rested on my shoulder. I turned around and began shivering as I looked the teacher in the eye. Why would he touch me? He should have just said my name to get my attention. From the corner of my eye, I could see Aaron turn around and stare at both of us. He looked between both of us but didn't leave the room. I was thankful for that. I needed a witness to what was about to happen to me. I needed someone to believe me.

"I would like to see you after school," he said. I nodded my head and darted once he let go of my shoulder. I even whipped past Aaron without even realizing it.

"Tanner!" he yelled after me. I turned to him but kept walking as fast as I could until I reached the bathroom. I slammed my stall door closed and let my heart return to its normal beat.

I could do this. This teacher had no reason to do anything to me. Neither did the other one but he still did it and I let him. I placed my sweaty palms on my forehead and closed my eyes. I was much more prepared if something happens this time. I take boxing and am much stronger than I was last year. I would know the signs and get out of there before he could do something. If I got any weird vibes from him, I would leave. I would be proactive this time. I would stop it.

Collecting my thoughts and hearing a warning bell, I breathed out deeply and walked away from the stall door. I walked at a normal pace to lunch and solemnly sat by myself as I usually did. I watched around me as girls laughed and guys made snide comments. I watched as girls rolled their eyes at their best friend and guys checked the population out. I watched and observed.

That's what I'm best at. I've always been.

***

As I came home crying once again, I couldn't help but notice both of my parents' cars were in the driveway. This only meant one thing and I knew that my assumption was right. We were moving once again and I was thankful. This had to be the best timing ever. After what he did to me, I don't think I'd ever want to set foot in a classroom with another male teacher ever.

After he touched me and I cried out, he slapped me for being too loud. I just can't handle seeing him ever again so I was thankful when I went upstairs and saw my mom and dad packing. Their faces were red which meant that they had been determined to pack up before Luke or I had gotten home. It felt relieving that I could just start packing up my room too. We'd probably leave by Sunday which wasn't far away since today was Friday.

I wiped at the tears in my eyes when I passed my parents and closed my door behind me. No use in starting drama when we were just going to leave it behind in a couple of days. Being alone in my room made me feel safer to have tears in my eyes. I sobbed as silently as I could so that my parents couldn't hear me. I didn't want them to become alarmed. I thought that I could trust my

AMY KULP

teacher again. He hadn't done anything in months. What had gotten into him? Why did he just suddenly attack me like that?

He only hurt my back and my cheek so I felt lucky. When he slammed my back against the table, I knew there had to be a bruise from the roughness of it. Being slapped across the face had stung, but it didn't leave any marks on my body. I was extremely uncomfortable during the encounter and he explored my body, but it wasn't physical pain I endured. It seemed as if he was more curious about what my body was like. Even now, it wasn't the physical pain or the sexual pain that haunted me. It was everything he said during it. His mental games. He knew how to wear me down. After all, I had spent months bonding with him. He knew about my family. He knew about my friends. He knew about my Tanner.

He knew how each of them was my weakness.

He had threatened them. He had threatened my grades. He threatened to blackmail me. He threatened to make me a social outcast. He threatened that he could hurt me more or get me in the classroom by myself even longer. He told me that no one would believe me. He told me that my lies would just ruin his career. He told me that I was coming onto him. After all, there was no proof that he asked me to do these extra credit assignments. I was just some lonely girl who asked for assistance and did everything I could to impress him.

I let myself cry as I remembered how I couldn't fight him to get away. How my wrists were clamped under *his weight and my back was hurting so bad as he pinned me to the table. I couldn't even move out of the grasp and even though I attempted to kick him, my leg strength wasn't enough. His body weight was bigger than mine. I was too weak compared to him and nothing I did affect him.*

As I sat there contemplating how to better protect myself, the only suggestion that came into my mind was one that Tanner had given me multiple times: boxing, self-defense classes, karate, martial arts, something. I was against violence, but if it meant that I could protect myself from having this happening again, I was all for it.

I was all for it.

***

"A t-tutor?" I questioned softly, inching towards the door every second I was in the classroom alone with him. "Why do I n-need a t-tutor?" I whispered questioningly. I stepped back by the door again and grasped the handle with my fingers, just in case. The teacher pressed his lips together tightly and I watched his eyes linger on my hands.

"Is there something you want to talk to me about, Chloe?" he asked. I gulped and nodded my head no. He was the only teacher to call me Chloe because I was too much of a wimp to ask him to call me Tanner. He sighed and rubbed his hands on his forehead. "We have a counselor if you need someone to talk to." I nodded my head no again and I turned the handle on the door. "Don't worry, I picked a student tutor out. They usually help out more because students are less intimidated by their peers." I opened the door and watched as his forehead creased. "Chloe," he whispered. The soft tone of his voice made me worry and I took a step out of the door. "Chloe! Get back here. Don't walk away while I'm talking to you!" he yelled. I stayed frozen and I felt my body begin to shake. As I stood there, the shakes were just going to intensify. "The tutor should be here at any minute and then you could study wherever. In school, out of school, the bleachers, I don't care. But you will be studying Monday, Wednesday, and Friday. I have already set it up with your parents and they agreed to it."

I was a little taken back that he had spoken with my parents before me. He didn't give me a chance to redeem myself without my parents knowing. Maybe this was how teachers were supposed to handle situations. Maybe they were supposed to go to my parents first and talk about how best to handle the situation. I crinkled my eyebrows as I looked at him in a different light than my normal teacher. Maybe he was a good guy?

I was snapped out of my thoughts when Aaron came into my view. He ran down the hall and eventually, he stopped near the teacher and me. He was panting from the small run, but I wasn't sure why. He ran more at the gym and at times, he outran me at the gym. In either of those instances, he was barely ever out of breath. Maybe he was putting on a show that he was wimpier than he actually was. He wanted to surprise them. It was a good technique if that was his true intention.

"I'm here," he said, panting. He stared at the teacher and then towards me. "Am I tutoring Tanner?" he questioned. The teacher stared at him with a blank expression. The best description of the expression was when you thought something was common knowledge and it turned out that it wasn't. He shook his head no and gestured towards me.

"Her name is Chloe." Aaron looked at me weird for a moment and then he looked back at the teacher to correct him. He shook his head as well.

"She prefers Tanner, though."

"Is this true, Chloe?" the teacher asked. They both looked back at me and I felt the pressure to answer. I slightly nodded my head but they both registered it. The teacher immediately went back to his desk and I saw him scribble on a sticky note. "You should've told me the first day." He smiled over at me like he was relieved he knew this now. "Okay, Tanner." The teacher then took Aaron to the side to have a private conversation with him. I excused myself to stand out in the hallway. If they wanted me to know, they would tell me.

Once they were done talking, Aaron walked out of the classroom and faced me. He smiled at me, but I could barely muster one back. He showed me the books he had in his hands and I knew that he was ready to start our tutoring session. For a couple of seconds, I followed him aimlessly. However, as I got further and further behind him, he latched onto my wrist and dragged me with him. He probably knew I was trying to procrastinate. I was just wary of going anywhere alone with Aaron though. While I had been alone with him in multiple places, I didn't want him to get used to that happening. He could do something to me if he thought I was comfortable with him. He could take advantage of me - he was tougher, he was better at boxing, and he looked innocent. Who would believe me over him? I already had the reputation of being a bully.

"I know the perfect place to study," he said. "It's nice and quiet and not too many people know about it." I felt the panic in me begin to rise and I managed to stomp my feet to the ground. This got Aaron's attention as he had to recoil when I wouldn't move any further but he expected me to. He looked behind him and let go of me before asking, "Tanner?"

"Can we just do it at school?" I whispered. I looked over at the library and noticed that there were still some people hanging out in there. I wasn't sure whether it was detention, after-school activities, or the librarian but it looked like there would be people there. Besides, a library was where you were supposed to study and concentrate too. It was perfect for studying. I also just didn't want to tell him that I didn't want to be alone with him. How rude was that? "I feel... safer."

"Safer?" Aaron questioned, following me into the library. "Tanner, you don't think I would do something to you, do you?" he asked. I didn't answer as I walked to a table in the back corner. It may have been further away from the public eye but it was also quieter over here. He wouldn't be able to get away with shenanigans over here but I wouldn't be distracted if we studied over here. It was a win-win situation. Aaron followed behind me and took the seat opposite me. He still looked like he wanted an answer though. I felt my breathing become shaky from taking charge and I urged myself to calm down. I just had to think of calm thoughts. "Tanner?" I didn't look up when he spread his books, pencils, and papers out. I needed to focus on relaxing. "Are you okay?" I forced myself to fake a smile and nodded my head as I looked near him. I still couldn't make eye contact though. "Seriously, you could tell me."

"I'm fine," I stated. "Let's just… start studying," I whispered. Aaron nodded his head but I could tell that he was still curious about the subject.

He instructed me to read what we were currently doing in class but I still wasn't able to comprehend it. Even when I did all of the homework and read everything, I wasn't able to understand and translate the passages. In class, it was especially hard because I couldn't concentrate. I had to constantly wonder if I was going to have to defend myself. I read it silently and as soon as he asked me a question about it, I couldn't answer him. I thought that I understood what I was reading, but how do I read between the lines? How can I guess what the author is trying to say? I could tell that Aaron was frustrated with me though. So I tried to reread the passage but when he asked me the same question, I still didn't know the answer.

"Can I ask you a question?" he wondered. I shrugged my shoulders as I closed the book. Maybe a little distraction would work in my favor. "Why don't you like being called Chloe?" My body froze at his curiosity. He had never dared to push a question like that onto me before. With him breaking this boundary, I realized that we were slowly becoming closer to each other. I wasn't sure if it was as acquaintances or as friends but I didn't know what to tell him. I didn't like making close friends because they became curious. They asked questions. I didn't know how to answer the ones that I didn't want to answer.

In response, I just shook my head at him. He should know not to intrude in my life. I was done with the study session so I grabbed my books and started walking away from him. If our studying consisted of him asking me personal questions, I wanted a new tutor. I would never learn from him. He immediately got up and placed a hand on my shoulder. I tensed up and stopped and he turned me around with a slight push.

"You didn't have to answer the question but we still have to study," he said. I looked around again at the library. It was getting busier and I realized that even though we just left our table, some other group had already taken it. Whether it was because of clubs, athletics, or studying, more people were now crowding in here. "You want to go to my secret place?" he asked.

I nodded my head.

Aaron slowly walked me out of the school. Any time he got too far ahead of me, he turned around to make sure I was coming. Each time, he met my gaze and smiled at me. We walked to the parking lot and when he opened his passenger seat, he threw his books in. He then gestured for me to get in the front but I just stared at him. I didn't budge when he asked me to get in and it dawned on him that it wasn't an option for me to get in his car. He closed the door and got his stuff out again.

"I guess we could always walk."

I nodded my head in agreement. There wasn't going to be another option but I would let him think he made the decision. We walked further up the dirt lot until a steep incline was noticeable. While all students parked in a dirt lot, I could see that cars were rarely on this part of it. A car could fit up here but a truck would not. It was too narrow of a space. If someone wanted to bring their car up, they would have to be a decent driver because I would have hit the trees that swooped too close. He gestured for us to walk up to it and I was not ready for the incline. I felt my calves grow hard from the determination and I felt sweat beginning to develop on my forehead. This was a workout itself.

The walk was peaceful though. Aaron was trying to talk to me but I was too busy with my thoughts. He was different from other people I have met. While others would grow annoyed with my constant emotional state and back and forth between what I was comfortable sharing and what I wasn't, he remained calm. While I could tell that he did get confused with my behavior, he was patient with me.

"Can I ask you a question?" I stopped on the trail and watched as he turned to me. He looked at me with concern on his face and nodded his head wearily. "Why are you trying to be my friend?"

He stared at me for a moment before continuing to walk up the trail. I walked up with him to see if he would answer. When we made it to the top of the hill, I knew we were at his study spot. There was a guard rail to help protect whoever was dumb enough to walk too close to the edge. Aaron rested his arms on it and leaned forward as he peered out at the scenery. I could tell why he wanted to come here. There wasn't much noise except the wind blowing through the trees. While I could see the roads down below, the people looked smaller and I couldn't hear the traffic. Even if Aaron were to drive up here, I wasn't sure where he would park. The hill came to an abrupt halt and I don't believe his parking brake would have prevented his car from rolling backward.

When the wind blew again and I shivered, I stopped staring at nature. I looked around to find Aaron and saw him sitting down near a more grassy patch - further away from the guardrail. I joined him as he set out the textbooks, notebooks, and everything else we needed. I would need to make a mental note to bring a blanket next time - I hated the feeling of grass on my legs.

"It's beautiful up here," I mumbled. I opened my textbook to the page he was on and he agreed with me.

"Yeah, I come up here when I need to get away," he said.

"Get away?" I asked curiously.

He nodded his head but I wasn't going to pry. I didn't like when he did it to me so I wasn't going to do it to him. If he wanted to tell me, he would. If he didn't, I had to respect that. Although, it would be lying if I said I didn't want to know. I could only speculate.

Bullies possibly.

"From my family," he whispered.

Oh.

I stared down at the textbook in front of me but now it felt like a bad time to study. Should I say something about myself? It felt only fair. I didn't know what to say though. Were we even friends? I looked over at him and saw that he was staring at me. He didn't look away and for a second, I truly felt like I could trust him.

"Is that why you take boxing?" I asked. He stared at me but I saw that he was confused. "To protect yourself too?"

"What?" He shook his head and grabbed the open textbook from the ground. "Tanner, it's a job that pays decently." He shrugged his shoulders and his cheeks grew rosy. "Not everyone is as rich as you, okay?"

I just blinked at him. He was starting to get a little defensive but I hope he knew that I wasn't judging him. I tenderly reached out to touch his knee with my hand to show I was there for him. He didn't move my hand out of the way but I saw a faint smile appear on his lips. He placed his hand on top of mine and slowly took it into his. I allowed this and watched as his movements slowed down to comfort me.

"I'm sorry, that was rude of me." He shook his head and looked up at me. "We should study."

"Right." I took my hand away from his and listened to his instructions. It was easier to concentrate here than in the library. However, I wanted to know more about Aaron. I was glad that he shared that little bit of information with me but now I wanted to know more. Was that bad of me? Was it intrusive? Was it greedy? "Are you going to be okay?" I asked as I interrupted him mid-sentence. He looked at me for a second before questioning me back.

"Are you?"

"I don't know."

Aaron only nodded his head. He didn't try to push me. He didn't try to pry into my life. I appreciated that. He was learning and it showed he cared. Maybe he wanted to be my friend. Did I want to be his?

"Oh, excuse me, my uncle is calling." He paused as he pulled out his phone and looked at the caller ID. He nodded his head at me before getting up. "Reread that passage and try to decipher it line by line."

I nodded my head as he walked near the rail guard. While I was able to pick up on everything Aaron said, I attempted to keep to myself. I needed to focus.

While it was great that Aaron was seeming more like a friend than someone I knew, I needed a tutor to help me study. I needed to focus on my studies. I did not want to fail. If I failed, the teacher would try to tutor me. I didn't want to think about what would happen if he tutored me.

As he paced back and forth, I couldn't help but watch him. My eyes lingered as his fingers ran through his hair and as he turned away from me. I decided that if Aaron wanted to, I would be his friend. I know that he was asked to tutor me so I shouldn't consider this hanging out. However, I had to remember all of the times he tried to be helpful. All of the times that he had stopped to say hi or tried to talk to help me at the gym. I couldn't forget about the time that he tried to give me a ride. The realization immediately hit me that we were closer than I originally thought.

I had a friend.

"Hey, Tanner, do you mind if we come back to this Wednesday?" he asked. He scratched his neck and came back over to me. "My Uncle Craig has been traveling from Georgia to come and help out on the weekends." He looked at me to see if I was judging him but I only felt myself getting colder from the temperature. "He's just arriving so I wanted to meet him at home." I nodded my head and looked back down at the textbook. "Don't worry though, it won't be a consistent thing. He's a science teacher so he knows that education is important."

While I'm sure that Aaron meant well, I couldn't comprehend what he was saying. My brain started swirling. I started putting pieces together of who he was talking about and felt myself beginning to shake. I absentmindedly reached for my necklace and bit my cheek when I didn't have it.

Uncle Craig.

Who's a science teacher.

From Georgia.

That sounded like my ex-teacher Craig Moore.

Who's a science teacher.

From Georgia.

Chapter Eleven

"Hey, you!" I turned around and pushed my glasses up the bridge of my nose. Were they calling for me? When I saw that it was Luke's friend, I had to assume it was. I groaned since his friends always picked on me when Luke wasn't around. "I heard about the…" He pointed to his neck but I pretended I didn't know what he was talking about.

In truth, I was petrified of what this conversation was going to lead to. I didn't think that Luke would tell anyone about the hickeys on my neck. The worst I feared was that our parents would find out and give me a talk about safe sex. As annoying and embarrassing as that would be, I would rather that than Luke telling his friends about them. At this point, I don't want a boyfriend. The students here were not as good as Tanner and the fear of what might happen to me had multiplied. Someone who wasn't my boyfriend forced those upon me. What would my boyfriend do?

"The hickeys," he said loud enough to get stares from the other kids. He suggestively raised his eyebrows up and down at me and I was able to read between the lines here. I made a disgusted face at him to show that I wasn't interested. If Luke were to find out about this… I stopped my thought there. If it wasn't for Luke breaking his promise to me, I wouldn't have them.

"What do you want from me?" I questioned.

The boy quickly grabbed my arm as if I had said the magic words. He rushed me into the stairwell when he heard the bell and I gulped as students were no longer going up and down the stairs. They were now going into their classrooms. We were going to be alone. My feet dragged along with him as I was tripping over myself but he didn't stop nor slow down for me to fix myself. He sat on the ledge that was behind the stairs and stared at me.

"So who gave them to you?" he wondered. My mouth started speaking without my mind's permission but I quickly stopped myself from saying too much. "Eh, not trusting me? Because I'm your brother's friend?" he questioned. I shrugged my shoulders and watched as he pulled a lighter and cigarette out. He offered me one but I denied it. "I'm just warning you that you don't want a bad name in this town or school. So many pervs will come up to you and beg you for a trip to—"

"I'm still a virgin," I blurted. He only laughed at me.

"Obviously. You're too pure and innocent to do anything active. Hell, I'm even surprised you have the marks on your neck." I wiped my hand across my neck and realized my mistake. I stared at my hand when the foundation came off and his eyes grew big. "Wow, there's a lot too." He looked intently at my neck and when I started getting uncomfortable, he stopped staring. "I'm just saying that you have a bad reputation because Luke's been telling everyone he meets about the marks."

"Really?"

"Well, no. He told his girl and she's telling everyone."

I felt steam come out of my ears as he mentioned Luke's girlfriend. If she wasn't at my house with Luke, I wouldn't have these marks. I wouldn't be afraid to go to school. I wouldn't be afraid to go to class. I wouldn't be afraid of him. I didn't know which girl I was mad at though. He had too many for me to pinpoint which one was at the house that day. When I heard his and my name being called over the intercom, he burned his cigarette out. "You coming?"

Since this was my science teacher period, I didn't really want to go. "Not today." Luke's friend just shrugged his shoulders and sat back down. "Can I tell you something?" I asked.

"Shoot."

"Well, first I need you to promise you won't make any rash decisions and tell anyone."

"What kind of trouble are you in?" he asked nervously. I waited for him to answer. I didn't move and didn't indicate anything to him. He eventually nodded his head nervously.

"You want to know how I got these hickeys?" He nodded his head and I felt myself sigh.

He was the first person I told.

He was the only person I told.

He was the only person who laughed before telling me that I had a wild imagination.

AMY KULP

He was the reason I never told Luke.

He was the reason I never told my mom.

He was the reason I never told my dad.

He was the reason I never told anyone.

He was the reason I became stone-cold.

He was the reason I couldn't talk to a boy without a stutter because he would mock the way I talked. He would make me repeat myself twenty times before laughing with Luke.

Of course, it didn't help that I told his nephew that.

Of course, he was going to believe that his uncle was innocent.

Of course, he got mad at me for speaking my truth.

Of course, he wanted his revenge.

Of course, he treated me ten times worse.

Of course, Luke just let it happen.

***

"Tanner, can I talk with you?" Aaron asked as he sat at my table. I looked over to where Aaron usually sat and saw his buddy's glance. Their stares immediately turned back to each other after a couple of seconds of shock. I turned my attention back to Aaron and nodded my head no. To get away from him, I got up and dumped my lunch tray. I wasn't done yet but I immediately lost my appetite seeing him. Seeing who he resembled. Seeing who he was related to.

I walked into the hallways without another word to him. I wasn't sure where I was going until I was already in the school gym. Technically, nobody was supposed to be here during school hours. I didn't care if I got in trouble though, I just wanted my release from my anger and sadness. I started up a treadmill and instantly began running on it. No point in warming up. No point in changing into the appropriate clothes either.

Aaron. I couldn't comprehend how his uncle was my science teacher. While I didn't ask him about it, I knew it had to be the same guy. The more I looked at him, the more I saw it. They looked alike. They talked similar to each other. It had to be the same guy. How many Craig Moore's lived in Georgia? What did that mean about Aaron? Aaron was someone I was just starting to trust. How could I possibly trust him now? He was probably in cohorts with his uncle. He knew where I was heading and realized he had a nephew there to ruin my life. What's a more perfect way to ruin my life than by making me trust someone? He probably took the tutoring position so that he could do something to me. He would probably make sure I stayed quiet about his uncle. After all, that's what his other nephew did.

The way he talked to me made me feel as if he cared.

I just can't trust him.

I just can't trust anyone anymore.

No Summer.

No Luke.

No mom.

No dad.

Just me.

Even as I was spiraling, I knew that I was being ridiculous. Why would Aaron try so hard to be my friend if he was working with his uncle? Usually, when I shrug people off, they don't try to be my friend again. They don't take up tutoring to help me. They don't keep pushing to let them in. Why did Aaron try so hard?

I increased the speed on my treadmill as I felt the burn in my lungs. I needed to do this. I was perfectly fine with being by myself anyway. I was doing fine up until now. I didn't need Aaron. I just need to have a good head on my shoulders and then hopefully I could make it through high school and onto college. I just needed to count on myself.

If I counted on someone else, they would just let me down and I honestly didn't need that right now.

Hearing the bell ring to indicate the ending of lunch, I slowed the treadmill down and shook myself out. I dampened my face for a second before trudging out of the gym. I made sure no one saw me leave or enter and walked calmly to my locker. I just had to get through the rest of my classes. Aaron wasn't in any of them and it was pretty easy to avoid him. I didn't catch sight of him until dismissal.

"We still have to study together."

I turned around and ignored him. I didn't have to do anything with him. I walked past him without a word and pretended I didn't see him. If I had to stoop this low, I would. I was not going to let myself get hurt again.

When will Aaron learn to stay away from me? I wasn't good for him. If he wanted to be friends, acquaintances, romantically involved, or just a training partner. I wasn't good for him. I was too mentally unstable. I was cool one second then I was heated nee xt. I was ready to let go of my necklace in one situation but needed it the next. I was content now but crying later.

I was not okay.

Chapter Twelve

"Tanner," I whispered. He ushered me over by the grass that he was sprawled onto and I looked at the picnic basket on the blanket. I smiled at him and sat right next to him, not minding the stares that we were getting from other people. It might've been weird to have a picnic on the front lawn of the school but I honestly couldn't find it any more romantic. "This is so nice," I whispered into him and lightly pecked his lips.

"Is Summer coming?"

"She said she was but I haven't seen her," I said. At that time, I looked around but didn't see her face in sight. "Do you think she just wanted to leave us alone for the day?"

"Yeah, she doesn't like it when we get all sappy on each other." I smiled and nodded my head as he pulled out two sandwiches. As he took his first bite, I took mine too but my thoughts were on something else. Since I was as readable as an open book, Tanner immediately knew something was up and quietly asked so nobody else could hear him. "Is there something wrong?"

"Have you ever thought about if..." I paused for a moment and shook my head. "Never mind. It's stupid. I'm stupid." I bit into my sandwich but I couldn't get the thought out of my head. As Tanner realized that talking was useless, our picnic turned out to be a silent period

and when he started packing up, I helped him so it was quicker. "I'm going to go find Summer."

Tanner nodded his head and we both dispersed into different areas of the school. I walked slowly to my locker and listened for the bell to ring. As it did, I set off to the gym lockers and was happy to realize that Summer was in my next period. Thankfully, I wouldn't have to hunt for her and thank her because we always talked during gym.

When I finished changing and still noticed that Summer wasn't in the changing room, I instantly grew concerned. Summer would never miss a class—no matter how much she sucked at it. Waiting for the rest of the girls to disperse, I quietly walked around the changing room to realize she wasn't even in here.

Knowing that I would eventually get in trouble, I thought about the choices I possibly had to gain or lose from it. Rolling my eyes, I took the chance and wandered the halls to find out where Summer was. I first checked all empty classrooms, bathrooms, and any small place that Summer could possibly be. When I came up empty-handed, I traveled around the halls aimlessly and jolted when I heard a whimper.

Seeing a body down the hall walking towards me, I ran towards it. It didn't even matter if it was Summer or not because I just wanted to help this soul. When I neared the person, I realized that it was indeed Summer. Although I was to expect that Summer was crying, I didn't expect her to have a bloody nose. It was gushing and I knew that she was beaten up.

They had never physically harmed her before.

Instant fear washed over me and I ran to her like my life depended on it. As I asked questions to her, she refused to answer and continued to walk to the nurse's office. She quietly tiptoed to the room and right before she got in, I grabbed her arm. I dragged her to the bathroom with me and figured that we could take care of her nose there. She wasn't telling me something and it was bothering me. What was the nurse going to do differently than us? "Summer, what's wrong?"

"Nothing." I was taken back by the sudden roughness in her voice. She kept her nose pinched as I gave her paper towels to dab it with. "It's just that when I needed my two best friends the most, they were probably making out on their blanket."

"Summer..." I put my hand on my forehead and felt my face flush. "We thought you wanted us to have alone time." How could I be stupid enough to believe that? I should have known something was wrong. I should have followed my gut.

"Why?" she harshly asked, whirling on me. "So you guys can leave me in the shadows as you get closer?" She turned back and unclenched her nose. It seemed to stop bleeding so she dabbed at it before washing her face. "I love both of you but I'm starting to feel like a third wheel around you guys and I hate it."

We walked together in silence back towards our class period. I'm sure we wouldn't be yelled at if I explained the situation. Teachers knew about the bullying. School counselors knew about the bullying. Most of the time, they tried to help. However, the help usually backfired and they would taunt Summer even more. I let her change and my mind began wandering. Was my first theory right? I couldn't help but blurt it out when she started tying her shoes.

"Do you like Tanner?"

"Of course, I do. He's my best friend."

"I mean... like boyfriend material."

It took a moment before Summer answered and I nodded slowly as she walked out of the room. I just let the answer sink into my skull for a moment and then sighed.

"Yes, I like him. But he chose you..."

***

"You know, you can't avoid your problems forever." I listened to Aaron blabber from behind me and sighed as I closed the notebook I was taking notes in. "You obviously stayed after school for the tutoring lessons still, so…"

I sighed and nodded my head no. "I'm studying on my own so just leave me alone," I said sternly. I might've looked intimidating but I felt like I was about to blubber like a baby. "So go home or whatever."

"You want to be left alone but you chose the study spot I showed you?" I tried to pay attention to what I was reading but I could see Aaron out of the corner of my eye. He sat down across from me and started opening his materials. I felt myself sigh before packing my stuff up. I must have been too slow because Aaron placed a comforting hand on my wrist to try and stop me. I felt myself beginning to relax for a second before seeing his face.

He looked so much like his uncle.

"Don't touch me."

I forced his hand off of me and instead of getting up to leave, I stood near the guardrail. Being able to see down below made me feel like I was in a hiding place. It felt like I could clear my head up here and I didn't want to give this place back to Aaron. My problems seemed so small up here. It felt like the longer I stayed up here, my problems wouldn't be eating me alive. I wouldn't have to fight off my thoughts when I'm alone.

Then again, that's what boxing was for.

"If you were trying to get away from me, coming to my hiding place wasn't a good idea." I expected him to sound angry at me but he sounded calm. He was calm. I just nodded my head - I didn't want to get into it with him. I didn't even mind that Aaron was right next to me as I continued to think. His presence felt comforting to me. I really wish it didn't though. "What's specifically on your mind?" he questioned.

I shook my head and he didn't pester me again. I was thankful for that. I was wondering if I should honestly tell him what was on my mind but before I could open my mouth, Aaron was the one to decide to speak first.

"So I have news." I had no idea what he was talking about but I just let the wind blow my hair around my face and stared off in the distance. Aaron would open up if he wanted to and I didn't want to pressure him. I would show him the same respect that I wanted. "I'm moving." I looked at him from the corner of my eye. He was staring off too. Me being there didn't have any effect on him, he would have been up here anyway. "My mom and I just can't hold the fort down anymore. My Uncle Craig offered to take us in."

"What?" I squeaked. I turned to Aaron very fast and he seemed surprised. "You can't do that! You can't go live with him!" I felt petrified on the inside and Aaron seemed confused. He didn't even know that I knew his uncle from Georgia. I didn't tell him anything. Maybe he really didn't know. I couldn't let that monstrosity take Aaron away from me. I couldn't let him fall into the trap that I fell into.

"Tanner, is there something you want to tell me?'

I shook my head and grabbed my school supplies. I felt emotion start to build up inside of me. I'm not sure if it was anger or sadness. I couldn't control it right now and I didn't want Aaron to see me like this. I turned around hesitantly to see that he was staring at me. I'm sure he hated that I was making this about me. He wanted to vent to me. He wanted to be sad with me. I was making it about me again.

"Just please don't go."

I'm sure he heard because he sucked his cheeks in with thought. I couldn't do more than that. It wasn't directly a hint towards his uncle but it was pretty obvious. Aaron would hopefully take it as the way that we were friends and I didn't want to be left alone. Or that I liked him more than friends. I was even fine with that thought. I was fine with any thought if it meant he could stay.

But I wasn't directly sure of what he was thinking about.

I excused myself and rushed the rest of the way home. I didn't think about anything except burning away my emotions. They were disappearing. The emotions were slowly turning into the burning sensation in my lungs and calves. I didn't stop though. I didn't take a break from the run until I was home. I stopped just short of my house to see that my mom and my dad's car were in the driveway. Neither of them was usually home at this time.

Were we leaving? Usually, we stayed somewhere for a year. It would be odd to stay less than that. Especially since I didn't want to move. It was an odd sensation to feel again. Last time I had felt this was with Summer and Tanner. I barely had anyone here though. I had Missy, my gym, and Aaron. I wouldn't consider us friends yet but I cared enough about him that I didn't want him to move in with his uncle.

"What are you doing home so early?" I questioned as I got through the door. I placed my textbooks on the table and watched as they both jumped apart from each other. They looked like they had been caught stealing a cookie from the cookie jar.

"What are you doing home so early?" my mom asked. "Aren't you supposed to be tutoring with that boy from your gym?"

"Normally." I grabbed an apple from the fridge and continued to stare at them. "He canceled it because he had a family emergency to tend to." I shrugged my shoulders and wondered how I had become so good at lying. I swear I used to be bad at it. Now I was lying to my parents about everything. Were they going to lie to me too? As I bit into my apple, I secretly wondered what they were hiding. When I came into the kitchen, they were whispering in hushed voices and they were crowded around each other; that's a little suspicious.

I just nodded my head when they didn't give me an answer to the first question I asked. I gave up on them. I was tired of people wanting me to intrude and pry into their lives. That wasn't who I was. Maybe a couple of years ago I would have been okay with that but not anymore. Everybody had secrets and if they wanted to tell them, they would. I trudged up to my room and stared at the ceiling as I lay on my bed. My mind started wandering over to Luke since he was the only one who hadn't come home early. He usually always had someone here when he thought that no one would be there.

Looking for what time it was, I slowly crept off of my bed and grabbed my phone. Time passes when you're avoiding your tutor and staring off into space. Apparently, I stared off too long because I was over thirty minutes late to the gym. I hurried to pack my gym bag and walked out of my room.

"Mom, I'm going to the gym!" I screeched.

"Okay!"

As I opened the door, I shut it loudly and waited a couple of minutes so they would think I was gone. Would this actually work? I've seen it in movies but I've never tried it. Maybe it would work because they had no reason to think I would be listening in on their conversation. I didn't seem interested before, why would I be all of a sudden? Sneaking quietly to the kitchen, I listened from the hallway. If they were seated where they were before, they wouldn't be able to see me from their view.

"But we can't tell her that, exactly."

"Well, the next time she skips the gym—"

Luke has great timing. As soon as the door opened, my mom got out of her seat to greet Luke. He immediately went upstairs but she stared at me instead. I stared back and did a cutesy type of smile. I cleared my throat and went the rest of the way to grab a bottle of water. It's the best excuse I could come up with on the spot.

"I needed water," I whispered.

As soon as I grabbed the water bottle, I placed it in my bag and took off. I knew they were talking about me and they knew that they were caught. I'm just glad that she didn't make a big deal out of it. It was clear that they were talking about me going to the gym. Or that I haven't been going as much. I felt a little betrayed though. Usually, my mom or my dad talked to me about this sort of thing first. Anything that bothered them, they would talk to me.

It still surprised me to think that they could keep secrets. I knew that everyone had secrets but it was weird to think about your parents having them. Aaron had secrets. Summer had secrets. My mom and dad had them. I did. Luke probably did but I hadn't found out about them yet. Why couldn't people be more straightforward? Why couldn't I?

The only reason I could think of me not telling is that nobody would believe me. There was no camera evidence. It was his words against mine. I didn't talk to anyone afterward. I wasn't physically hurt. The one person I told didn't even believe me. Sometimes I think that I imagined everything but then I remember that I didn't.

Because Luke saw the hickeys.

And yet, he didn't even tell our parents. He didn't even investigate the subject. He saw them, told his girlfriend, told his friends, and then did nothing. A caring older brother would've done something. An overprotective brother would've done something. A brother would've done anything.

Luke did nothing.

AMY KULP

Chapter Thirteen

"Who would believe you?" I closed my eyes and felt his breath on my neck. "You're just a loner girl that everyone knows is from another state. You're overshadowed by your brother. Your brother that everyone likes." I closed my eyes tighter as I felt his lips come closer to my neck and I managed to suppress a whimper. "Everyone likes your brother. Except you and everyone can see that. If you say anything, they'll just think you're lying so you could have something your brother won't have—a scandal." I licked my lips and turned my head away from him as he sank his nails into my arm. "Or is it because you feel betrayed? Because he picked his girlfriend over his own sister." Shivers went down my spine as he made me look at him. "Don't you get it, Chloe? Only one person loved you and that was Tanner but he's not here. Nobody cares about you and nobody would believe you. Am I right? What did your brother do when he saw the hickeys?" he asked. He tightened his grip on me until I couldn't take it anymore.

"H-h-he told his friends," I whispered.

"He what?"

"H-he—"

"A little louder."

"He told his friends..." I felt tears welt up in my eyes but I wasn't sure if it was because of what Luke did or because of the pressure on my hands.

"And what did his friends do to you?"

"M-mocked me."

"Hmm?"

"They made fun of me and joked around with me. Asked me where my corner was."

"What did your brother do?"

"He laughed along." I felt my back begin to shake and I couldn't control the tears that were escaping my eyes.

"I'm the only one here for you, Chloe."

I cried so hard when he placed his hand on my thigh and I wanted to swat it away but I know that he would just hit me or make it ten times worse.

"Knock, knock." The teacher jolted away from me as the person in the doorway stood still. They dropped their papers on the ground and his eyes darted between me and the teacher. A horrified expression was on his face and I felt more tears sliding down my cheeks.

Would his nephew believe me now?

***

"So what does that mean?" he asked me. I hit my pencil against my chin as I tried to understand the Greek poems. I shrugged my shoulders and Aaron simply sighed at me. We have been going at this for about an hour now.

Dissecting each line. Aaron had to tell me what each of them meant, I still wasn't sure. "You do have to try, you know?"

"I am," I simply replied. "But I don't even know if it's first or third person. It's all just dialogue." I flipped through the pages again and attempted to read when Aaron simply shuffled some papers into his book. I have never been so bad at a subject before. It felt pointless for me to keep trying.

"What's on your mind?" he asked. I closed my books and looked around at the other students and tutors. We opted to try and study in the library today so that I would be more concentrated. It didn't seem to be working. As there were quite a few people in here, I kept getting mildly distracted whenever someone walked past us. Aaron instantly knew what I was thinking because when he started packing up his bag, he lent me his hand. Without accepting it, we walked out of the school together and started strolling up his hill.

"So I guess this is now our secret spot instead of just mine." I didn't answer and just looked out in the view as Aaron attempted to read my face. "My mom and I talked about it, Tanner." I looked over at him but didn't know what he was talking about. "We aren't going to my uncle's."

I immediately smiled at him and was overjoyed with this outcome. I didn't know that my opinion had a say in what they were going to do. I just assumed Aaron was lost to me once he would move. It was so relieving to hear this. Caught up in the moment, I brought Aaron into a brief hug. As soon as we departed, it was awkward. He motioned to get set up on the ground and I got my stuff ready as well. I haven't hugged anyone in a while and it felt nice. It felt comforting. I couldn't comprehend the warmth I had felt from Aaron.

"I will have to pick up additional shifts at the gym though."

"What about our study sessions?"

"You'll have to find a new tutor," he softly replied.

"Or I could just come to the gym and study with you there?" I questioned. He looked over at me and nodded his head. I smiled at him as if that would convince him. He smiled back but shook his head again at me. Before he could protest verbally, I opened my mouth even further. "You could help me with my boxing too if you'd like."

"Good…" He smiled at me and I smiled back before turning back over to the view. "Because you have disgusting posture."

I couldn't help but let out a cackle in response. His laughter radiated through the small space and filled it up. It no longer felt peaceful and calm. Instead, it felt like a joyful and happy place. I'm glad that this dynamic was changing.

"You want to try reading it again?"

I shook my head no but opened up my textbook anyway. I grabbed the worksheet that we needed to fill out for homework and looked at the questions. We only had one filled out and it was mostly Aaron's answer that filled it.

"'How did Priam die?'" Looking through the textbook, I almost felt like throwing it over the edge. "Here." Aaron scooted over next to me and pulled the book into his lap. I stared longingly at the pages until Aaron pointed with his index finger. "Try and interpret this page. You'll find the answer in here somewhere."

I nodded my head and looked to see it. I must have reread the section twenty times before I closed my eyes and exhaled. How were people able to understand this?

"It doesn't matter how many times I read this, I don't understand it!"

"Tanner, are you okay?" Aaron looked at me with concern and my eye twitched towards him. "I know there's something bothering you."

"How would you possibly know that?"

"You haven't been to the gym in over a week." I pressed my lips together. Aaron was similar to me in that he noticed things. Whether it was how I was acting or how someone was texting, he would notice. He was similar to me. I tried to notice everything anymore. Especially with reading a room. "You've also been getting angry over little things." He gestured towards the book and continued, "You're a lot quieter than usual as well." He placed a reassuring hand on my shoulder and I felt like pushing it off. I kept it there though. "I've told you my story, what's yours?"

"I don't have one—"

"Everyone has one." Aaron shook his head slightly and smiled a bit. "It describes who you are. Like, why aren't you wearing that necklace anymore?" I looked down at my chest and put my hand to it.

"It belonged to my ex-boyfriend," I whispered. The atmosphere of the area changed again. I knew it was going to become somber. "He's dead." Aaron's face instantly softened but I could tell he expected more. I felt sweat beginning to develop under my armpits and I felt myself beginning to get nervous. This was unusual. I usually didn't get nervous around Aaron.

Did I care what he thought about me?

I opened my mouth to tell him more but heard a soft beeping. He immediately got up to turn it off but the moment was ruined. I knew that he had to start his shift at the gym soon. He slowly started packing his stuff up and I did too. We carefully walked down the hill together and when he got into his car, I called out his name.

"Yes?"

"His name was Tanner."

Chapter Fourteen

I was surprised at how easy they could talk about me behind my back. Down in the living room, my family was talking about me. Luke, mom, and dad. They were all talking about me because they all thought I was sleeping. I just happened to walk out of my room to go to the bathroom when I heard them say my name. I had to pause and listen because I was curious. Why would they be talking about me? I sat at the top of the stairs and attempted to not make a noise. I was just here to listen.

"She's not really coming out of her room anymore," my dad noted. "She's becoming antisocial."

"She's a teenager, it happens," my mom defended. I smiled knowing that I could count on my mom for my back. Besides, my mom would relate to me more because we were both females. My dad and I probably aren't going through the same crisis as me and my mom would. Although, I would never wish anyone to be going through what I am.

"She's already sixteen, anti-social stage happens during the fourteen-fifteen process," Luke stated. Of course, he would try to get my parents off of my side. He tried to find anything that was wrong with me so that he could have people against me. Why did he dislike me so much? He was rooting against me. "Does she even come

out for food anymore?"

"Not that I know of," my mom stated.

"No."

That was such a lie. I took food when nobody was home or when they were all sleeping. I would never starve myself. I would do a diet but never starve myself. My mom and I talked about how to get healthier. My fitness goal was to get more muscular and strong, not weak and frail. I wanted to be able to beat the next person who looked or touched me wrong.

"Well, she needs new hobbies and friends," my dad said. "The moving thing is probably hurting her more than doing her good. Let's put her in a club or something?"

"What does she like to do?"

"C-can I do b-boxing?" I questioned as I came downstairs. The look on everyone's face was satisfying to me. It was even more satisfying to know that they wouldn't have a clue that I was eavesdropping on their conversation before I interrupted. My mom instantly shook her head, yes and I saw her cheeks begin to blush. My dad didn't look as convinced but when my mom elbowed him in the stomach, he agreed. I shook my head with satisfaction and made my way back up the stairs. However, I couldn't help but hear what Luke had to say about me.

"What's with the stutter?"

***

"Your feet are too far apart," Aaron noted. I rolled my eyes and hit the bag twice before fixing my feet. "Good, do you feel a difference?" I barely nodded my head as I hit it again and Aaron looked down at the textbook as he recited something that I should repeat.

As he was teaching me and helping me with boxing, I noticed Missy hovering near the corner and peering over at us. I was quite interested in what she was doing but Aaron quickly knocked me out of my trance by flicking his fingers in my face. I needed to focus and I knew that it was about multitasking. He wanted me to focus on boxing while I was studying. I could barely study without the distraction. I'm not sure how this was going to work out.

"Come on," he said. I nodded my head and attempted to get in focus again but Aaron soon saw my distraction. He looked back behind him and he knew why Missy was staring at us. "She wants to talk to you once we're done."

I nodded my head and hit the bag multiple times before Aaron made me do the jump rope. I kept reciting what he wanted me to do and as I progressed in the lesson, he progressed my boxing skills. At one point, I was so focused on translating the passage, that I accidentally tripped myself with the rope. Aaron laughed at me and helped me up. I tried to control my laughter but soon I joined in with him. When my stomach began to ache from laughing, Aaron dismissed me so he could control himself as well. I was too distracted to study and he had to help train other people.

"You should probably see what Missy wants," Aaron said.

I nodded my head in agreement and started walking towards her. I felt my laughter begin to slow down and when I turned back to see how Aaron was doing, he was already coaching someone else. I mindlessly followed Missy into her office and sat in an empty chair she had. She remained quiet as she booted up her computer and I wasn't going to be the first to speak. I watched as she typed in what she needed before turning to me.

"Tanner, there are some things we need to talk about." My mind immediately flew to everything that I might've done wrong in her gym, ever. It was a long list but when Missy sighed, I immediately stopped thinking and turned to her. She wasn't one to prolong things so if she had a problem with me, she would tell me. "Your mom…" She shook her head for a moment and it seemed like she was going to cry since she pinched the bridge of her nose. "You can't do boxing anymore."

"Why?"

"Your mom says she's taking you out."

I knew that Missy wanted to say more to me but I didn't want to listen to it. I stormed out of the room and forced myself into the locker room. I felt my anger starting to bubble up in my body and knew that I wanted to hit something. I wanted to hit a punching bag. I wanted to work out. I wanted to run. I wanted to do something to get my mind off of the betrayal.

So I forced myself to take a calming shower.

Boxing was my safe haven. Boxing was my release. It let me get rid of all of my negative emotions in favor of keeping my positive emotions. It saved me when my mind was a black spiral and it saved me when I was new here. It helped me get social again and it helped me gain friends. It helped me feel at home and it helped me feel like I always had a second home if I needed it. Instead of becoming a victim, I was able to become a warrior here. I was able to repair the cracks that had formed in my armor. They were still there but it helped to temporarily fix them.

It hurt that my mom wanted to take that all away from me. Did she have a reason for it? I know she and my dad were talking about it because I wasn't going to it often. Since that talk, I have been more involved with it. My attendance has skyrocketed and I've been there almost every day. Aaron has been tutoring me here almost every day. Does she want my grades to suffer?

When I heard the locker room doors open, I shut down the water and quickly dried myself off. I didn't pay attention to who it was that was in here but it was enough to make me stop crying in here. I couldn't show emotion with other people around me. I grabbed my things and headed out of the gym.

I needed to talk to my mom.

When I had arrived home, I immediately noticed my mom's car. It filled me with more sadness and anger than I expected and my body started running towards the house. Why was she home so early again? As I stormed through the house, any anger in me vanished when I saw my mom's face.

Her face was pale and she was snuggling into her favorite blanket. While her hair was usually brushed into a perfect bun, it was tangled into a topknot. Her cheeks looked skinnier than I remember them and her glow that lit up a room was gone. She looked sick.

"Are you okay?" I asked. She nodded her head and opened up the blanket for me to join her. I took the seat next to her and she wrapped herself up again. I saw a small flash of hurt cross her face but it went back to her pale sad skin. Was she going to tell me the truth? Or was she going to change the subject like she's been doing the past weeks?

"I got laid off at work."

This explained so much. I was devastated for my mom because I knew how much she loved her job. However, I couldn't help but feel a little selfish as I wondered how this would affect me. I already got boxing taken away from me. Would we have to downsize? Would I need to get a job? Were we financially okay? I was a little excited though. This means I would be able to see her more. Maybe we could build a connection that I've always wanted. Maybe she was going to put family over work now.

Was my mom okay?

"What about dad?" I questioned. I rubbed her back

as she picked at the blanket and sniffled in response. "He's still working right?"

"Yeah." She nodded her hand and smiled slightly. "I need to find another job and you need to concentrate on your studies. While I'm not usually a stay-at-home mom, I will be until I get my job. So continue studying with Aaron and I will continue to overlook your grades."

"Mom, it's only one class."

"Yeah but you're failing it." I rolled my eyes but she didn't see as her face was turned to the ground. I could not argue with her when she was in this vulnerable state. "I should probably tell Luke the news."

"He's not home," I whispered.

"Probably out with his girlfriend."

"Wait, what?" I questioned. My back perked up and my eyebrows probably slithered down my face. "He has a girlfriend?" Mom nodded her head slowly and looked at me with confusion. "Why didn't he tell me? Usually, he brings her home."

"He said that you would attempt to ruin it for him or something." She bit her lip and looked like she wanted to continue talking but didn't dare slip a word out. She already said too much.

Well, that hurts. I don't recall doing anything to Luke for him to think that. I was known for disliking every girl he brought home but I had my reasons. He went through a girl every other week. How was I supposed to know if he actually liked them or just wanted to use them? How could I support the relationship when the girl acts dumb? He knew that Tanner meant so much to me and if he might've found a girl like that, then I wouldn't put myself between the relationship. Even if it was someone like his old ex-girlfriend who hated me, I wouldn't mind because I know how much it hurts to lose someone like that. If he would have just talked to me about a serious girlfriend he had, I wouldn't judge him so harshly.

Deciding that I needed to walk to get my mind off of things, I simply went towards the study spot. Since I no longer had boxing to help me with my emotions, the next best thing was the study spot. It was a calming and peaceful place. While it may not help me get rid of my angry emotions, it usually helped me forget. I was usually alone while I was up there so I couldn't accidentally take my anger out on anyone.

I had to think of what I might've done to Luke's relationship that made him hate me so much. That made him keep secrets from me where I would never keep my relationship a secret. Then again for all he knows, I did keep a secret relationship from him. I mean after he found out about the hickeys, he demanded answers that I wouldn't give because I didn't know how to answer or avoid his questions. He threatened to tell mom and dad but instead told his girlfriend about me and ruined my life. I gained a horrible reputation because of him. Granted, I don't think Luke would be able to stop the rumor once he heard about them but it would have been nice to hear that he stood up for me. Nobody stood up for me.

His best friend was the one who walked in on Mr. Moore touching me.

His best friend was the one who was related to Mr. Moore.

His best friend was the one I trusted with all of my secrets.

As I reached my spot in the peaceful night, I simply sat in the dirt and picked at any surrounding grass. I didn't remember to pack a blanket for me to sit on but since I was wearing pants, I couldn't feel the grass against my skin. I honestly just wanted to look up at the stars instead of the city but I couldn't put my brave face on to look up because I was frightened. Maybe I would be disappointed about the sky.

Everything has a way of disappointing me.

"Tanner, what are you doing here?" I slowly turned around and saw that Aaron was climbing up the hill. He had a flashlight with him since it was pitch dark around us and I shrugged my shoulders. "Do you want company?" he questioned.

I nodded my head and smiled as Aaron sat down. Even if I said no, I'm pretty sure that Aaron would still sit down. Although he doesn't bug me, he's very persistent about some things and that would've been one. I did want to be alone but I liked his company. I liked him. It made me feel comforted. It made me feel like I belonged here.

"I heard about the boxing." I nodded my head and looked up at him as he placed the flashlight on the ground. "You should ask Missy if you can work in exchange for the use of the gym."

"I don't want to be a bother," I whispered. "And plus I'm good at boxing but I can't even do my own posture. Never mind correcting other people's." Aaron smiled along with me and we both sighed at the same moment. "So, what are you doing here?"

"I always come here after I'm done with the gym," he replied. "It gives me enough courage to go in the house and take care of my mom." My face fell as Aaron looked up at the sky, something I have yet to do. "Can I ask you something?" I nodded my head a little skeptical and when Aaron looked back at me, I knew it was serious. "Why do you like being called Tanner?"

He asked me this before but I wasn't ready to answer it before. I wasn't even sure if I was ready to answer it now. I thought about what to say carefully. Truthfully, the reason was that I couldn't get Craig's voice out of my head. Every time he said my name, he clicked his tongue against his teeth as he whispered the C. The way he whispered it against my neck against me. The way he yelled at me. The way he treated me like a little kid.

Every time someone said my name, I couldn't help but feel prickles against my neck and I couldn't help but feel his hands on me. In places, nobody should touch unless they specifically had permission from me. I had never given permission before and he still touched me there.

"I just need a way to have my boyfriend back," I

whispered.

"You could've just kept the necklace, not just the name." I shook my head but I obviously confused Aaron as I choked up. "Do you mind if I call you it?"

"Please don't," I pleaded. Aaron nodded his head in understanding and drummed his knuckles on the cold hard ground. I knew that he didn't understand and was thankful he didn't push the subject any further. He was good with that. "So how are we going to study now?" I asked. Aaron shrugged his shoulders and for once, we were both speechless. "I really don't want to find a new tutor."

"Why's that? I remember the first time you would've killed to get a new one."

"You understand me," I whispered. When I looked up at Aaron, his face was blank and he was looking at me. I looked at him strangely and he did the same with me. "You're not too pushy or too relaxed. You understand that I need to bring my grades up."

Aaron nodded his head once before deciding to lay down in the dirt. I stared at his body for a moment before I did the same and laid down side by side with him. I stared at him for a while before looking to the sky.

It was beautiful.

"Tanner?" he asked.

"Hmm?"

"Why are you up here now?" he questioned. I breathed in and stared up at the sky speechless. Aaron didn't rush me. He knew that I heard the question. He didn't repeat the question because he was positive I was going to answer. And I knew I was too.

"I didn't want to hurt anyone in my family. I didn't want to yell at my mom or dad. I wanted to yell at my brother but he wasn't home so I… wanted to take it out on my mom. Instead, I stormed out and came to the only place I knew of."

"Why is that?"

"My brother told lies about me and my mom believed him." I shook my head and put my arms behind it. "It seems so stupid now." I shook my head again and felt childish explaining my emotions to him. Would he understand what I was feeling?

As we continued to sit in silence, I felt the temperature begin to drop. I could tell that Aaron was cold because as he moved in closer to me, I felt his coldness on the skin. I personally didn't mind since my mind was elsewhere but when I felt him shiver, I could tell he didn't want to leave me alone.

"I guess we should get going."

"Do you want a ride?" I bit my lip but nodded my head anyway. I grabbed the flashlight as we made our way to his car. He put the heat on for us and it felt nice compared to outside. My goosebumps slowly started to go away. When I sat in my seat, I buckled up and waited for him to begin to move. "Do you mind if I go to my place first? I want to check in on my mom."

I nodded my head and he drove out of the way. The car ride was long and quiet but I wasn't complaining since I was slowly getting sleepy as the time passed. Aaron remained seated when he parked and looked over at me once.

Not asking me to come with him, I stayed in the car and didn't think about getting out until I began to get cold again. Looking down at my cell phone timer, I could tell that it was very cold and very late out. I had been waiting in the car for about thirty minutes and Aaron still wasn't out.

Deciding that I should check on him, I let go of my seatbelt and pushed the car door open. The outside was cold so I wrapped my arms around myself and took note of his house. His house was very small but I could tell that Aaron has been cleaning it since the lawn was trimmed and there was no chipped paint. One thing I didn't expect to see was another car in his driveway.

I was one-hundred percent sure that Aaron said his mom didn't drive so I was a bit confused. Not caring, I walked up to the steps on his porch and stopped at the doorway.

Should I knock or go straight in?

I was about to knock when another thought struck my mind. What if his mom was sleeping? Silently agreeing to enter quietly, I cracked the door open and barely got the door closed since the wind was so heavy.

The inside of Aaron's house was dirty and dim. The smell of beer was relevant in the house and no lights were turned on except one. I didn't dare turn any on since I was afraid of waking up someone. I wasn't supposed to be here.

"Aaron?" I whispered. I didn't move until I knew my eyes wouldn't adjust any further from the darkness. I walked carefully in case his mother would be surprised and accidentally hit me. Technically, I am an intruder and had to be prepared for that. I walked towards the dimly lit room and stood in the doorway for a couple of minutes.

His mother was sitting in the recliner chair asleep. She looked rather peaceful except for the fact that around her were about twenty beer cars. I slowly wondered how they could afford this since they didn't have any money but it vanished when a hand slapped across my wrist and pulled me into the dark.

"What are you doing, Tanner?" Aaron asked, scared.

"I was starting to get cold so I came to find you," I whispered. I looked back at the recliner chair and when Aaron caught me, I saw the hurt cross his face. I didn't want to say anything but when Aaron held up a finger, I didn't object when he picked the beer cans up slowly and quietly.

"I'll be back, stay in the shadows," Aaron whispered. I nodded my head as Aaron disappeared with the beer cans.

Staying in the dark was kind of creepy though. It felt like I was spying on his mom and was hoping to rob their house. There wasn't much to rob but that didn't matter to me. I hated sneaking around.

It didn't help that Aaron seemed even more

freaked out than I was. He was jumpy and whispering like if his mom caught us, she would hurt me or him. That was what worried me and what worried more than anything was if he had a real reason to worry. Does she hit him? I know he told me, no but I wasn't sure if I should believe him. People that are being hit usually lie about it, right?

He also seemed embarrassed when he realized I had seen the inside of his house. I would hope by now that he wouldn't think I was materialistic. Aaron was a good person before and he would be the same person as I left him. I will admit I was judging how dirty and smelly his house was but I wouldn't let this change my opinion of him. It looked like he was the breadwinner of this house.

I instantly quieted my breathing down when I heard whispering from upstairs. Was there someone else here? Aaron told me it was only him and his mom.

After a couple more minutes, I couldn't help but wander through the living room and go up the stairs. I know that I should listen to Aaron but I couldn't help but get curious. Curiosity killed the cat…

Looking upstairs, I jumped half a mile when I heard a voice appear behind me.

"I thought Aaron said to stay downstairs." I knew that voice and I felt my whole body go tense. "You know he did it because he knew you didn't want to be near me." He put his hand on my shoulder and my whole body tensed. "Of course, he doesn't know why…" I felt his voice begin to trail off and I slowly turned around to face him.

Craig Moore.

My old school teacher.

Aaron's uncle.

"Wh-what are you d-doing here?" I questioned softly. His sickly smile appeared on his face as he took his hand off of my shoulder. "I-I thought A-Aaron wasn't…"

"Moving?" he questioned, finishing my thought. "Oh, he's not. He knew how uncomfortable you felt about the situation so I made some other plans and now I'm living here." He stepped closer to me and I attempted to shrink. When I was backed into the wall, he touched his finger to my chin. "You are just as pathetic as I left you."

"Don't," I attempted with courage.

"A little braver, but still pathetic."

"A-Aaron's somewhere up here…" I trailed off.

"Yeah, but I could convince him I wasn't doing anything either. Just like my nephew you told your brave, imaginative story to." I felt tears well up in my eyes as I remembered what he was talking about.

***

"I honestly don't believe you that much Chloe," he said. I looked at him strangely as we sat in the hallway stairwell. Why would I make something like this up? Who did he think I was? I wasn't doing this for attention and if he knew me at all, he knew the thing I would want the least is attention. "Not only is he a good teacher, but he's also been at this school for a long time. There would've been a

complaint by now if he was going to try something."

"You don't believe me?" I questioned.

"Why would I? You're just this random girl who moves every year." He shrugged his shoulders and stomped out his cigarette. "The girl who has hickeys on her neck and won't answer any of her brother's questions when asked about them. I'm pretty sure if he touched you in any way, you would've told your brother that the hickeys were from the teacher. Even if they weren't," he said. The bell rang and he looked back at me in sympathy. "I feel bad for people like you."

"People like me?" I wondered.

"People who have to ruin other people's lives to feel a spark in their own." He got up and turned around to stare at me. "Just because mommy or daddy pay more attention to their son than you doesn't mean anything." I was about to say something but he cut me off. "Just because Luke loves his girlfriend more than you doesn't mean anything."

"What—"

"I know. He told me." I must've looked confused because he just laughed at my face. "He told me how you were nervous about something and interrupted his and his girlfriend's important conversation." He put quote marks around important and I instantly knew they were just playing around. "You seemed stressed and for an instant, he was going to help you."

"How—"

"An instant, Chloe."

"B—"

"He was worried for you, for an instant. His first intention was to actually go with you." He took a step toward me and I looked at my hand. "He was afraid for you because he thought you sounded petrified."

"I-I—"

"But his girlfriend promised something better than the satisfaction of helping his little sister." I looked disgusted and he took another step toward me. He put his hands on my shoulders and pressed hard. I felt like yelling out in pain but I didn't dare. "The only reason you're spreading this story is that you're mad that he replaced you with her."

"T-That's n—"

"So, I find this a little pathetic. Especially since I see through your little game. How does it feel like starting rumors?" he asked. I felt my chin tremble. "I could start a rumor too. Especially about how you got those hickeys." My hand instantly flew to my neck. "How many hours do you work for your corner?"

When he started walking away, I stepped forward and grabbed his arm but he flung it back and looked at me jokingly.

"Like anyone would believe you anyway." As he opened the door to reenter the hallway and go to his class, he looked back once and laughed. "Don't spread rumors about my uncle."

***

AMY KULP

"I still feel so bad that he started that rumor about you though," he whispered. I shook my head and felt some tears fall down my face. "Although you have gotten more muscular." He squeezed my tricep and I jolted. "And prettier." He stroked my cheek with the back of his hand and I felt like crumbling inside. "I've been told you've been taking boxing lessons with Aaron."

I felt the tears fall down my cheek as I nodded yes while trying to hold down my voice. Although he still looked bigger than me, I still attempted to punch him in the stomach. He doubled over a little bit but that just gave me less room to escape from. I cursed myself under my breath since Missy always told us to hit them in their throat.

"Good try though," he said boxing me in the wall. "You still need much practice since you obviously don't do well under pressure." He chuckled a bit and looked behind him as he heard a door being closed. "You should probably go back in your hiding spot." He put his arms down so I could escape and laughed. "Aaron's coming so hurry."

I nodded my head and ran down the stairs as fast as I could. Not quietly though. I was surprised when I reached downstairs and saw that Aaron's mom was sleeping tightly.

She must've drunk a lot.

Going back in my hiding place, I felt myself hold in those escapable sobs. I felt the tears fall down my cheek and realized I still wasn't a match for him. I still couldn't hurt him if I tried. He always had an advantage over me.

Hearing Aaron's footsteps coming down the stairs, I attempted to stop my crying and hoped that Aaron wouldn't see the tear stains.

"Okay, Tanner."

I nodded my head and rushed ahead of Aaron and jumped in his car. Aaron was a bit dazed but didn't say anything as he turned the heat on and drove to my house. It was a while in the car and every time Aaron attempted to talk to me, I would just shake my head and stare out the window. I wasn't up for talking.

"Tanner, are you okay?" he asked. I nodded my head, yes and I knew Aaron had shaken his head in disbelief. "Did my mom do anything? I see tears in your eyes, on your face, and I see that you're trying to hold in sobs."

"Your m-m-mom didn't do any-anything," I sobbed. "She-she was sleeping the whole time."

"Are you stuttering again?" he questioned. I shrugged my shoulders and saw Aaron look at me from the corner of my eye. "I thought you stopped that." I shrugged my shoulders again. This must've infuriated Aaron because he pulled the car over the next possible time he could. "I'm not starting the car until you speak."

I remained silent and didn't talk until I began to shiver instead of sob.

"You didn't tell me your u-uncle was st-st-staying with you," I whispered. Aaron was appalled and turned

AMY KULP

fully towards me.

"You went upstairs?" he yelled at the top of his lungs. I wrapped my arms around myself and began shivering again. "I specifically told you to stay in your hiding spot!" he yelled. Tears were welling up in my eyes as he continued to yell at me. "I knew you would react like this! Everything I say has a reason to it, Chloe!"

My eyes turned big and so did Aaron's when he realized what he had just said. I instantly went full-blown crying out loud and I couldn't control myself.

"Tanner," he said softer. "Tanner, I'm sorry." He put his hand on my back and I instantly shook it off. "Seriously Tanner, I'm really sorry." I sniffled and attempted to stop crying but the way he said my name, sounded so much like how his uncle said my name. "But Tanner, I promise my uncle would never hurt me."

"Yeah but Aaron, he would hurt me," I whispered. I didn't mean to say it and it was so covered in sobs that I didn't even realize that Aaron had heard me. I said it so low that I didn't even hear it. I wasn't even sure that Aaron had heard me until he stopped patting my back and I finally looked up at him with tears streaming down my face like Niagara Falls.

"What do you mean, Tanner?" I shook my head and cried harder. "Tanner, what are you talking about?" Aaron scooted closer to me and put his arm over my body. I leaned into his chest and cried as he tried to soothe me. "Tanner, please you could trust me. I told you my story, let me hear yours."

"Aaron…" I whispered. "He molested me."

AMY KULP

Sitting at the top of the hill where Aaron and I should have been studying, didn't calm my nerves. This was supposed to be the place that helped me get away from everything. With Aaron not being in school the entire week, everything reminded me of him. Our tutoring sessions were a big part of why I was so concerned. For once, it wasn't just about me. I wasn't concerned about how my grades were probably slipping. I was worried about someone else besides myself. I was worried about Aaron. Especially since I knew about his predicament. Even with him missing school, I stayed at our spot just in case. In case he wanted to talk. In case he wanted to tutor me. In case he wanted someone to just be there for him. Just in case.

I sat on the dirt and listened to the sounds of nature mixed in with the sounds of busy cars. I've been so consumed with my worrying thoughts that I often didn't even answer my phone when it rang. I was in my own little world. I was too stubborn and focused on my thoughts to notice that it was ringing. My ears automatically tuned it out. After I got the dings of texts and multiple voicemails, I would realize who it was. My family called and was worried about me. I usually did them the favor of walking down the hill and coming home. They were probably frightened for me.

I wouldn't blame them.

This past week I haven't spoken a word to them. I come home very late and go upstairs to sleep. Then in the morning, I get ready without speaking to anybody and go directly to the school, usually an hour early to sit up on the hill. I eat breakfast and lunch at school but don't eat dinner since I get home very late. They probably assumed I wasn't eating at all. I didn't try to ease their minds about this though.

I don't know why they're worried about me though. I haven't seen a wink of Luke in forever. They don't seem too concerned about him though. I know that mom said he's been spending time with his girlfriend but sometimes he doesn't even come home. I guess they want him to grow up since it's his senior year and wants him to move out for college as soon as possible. I'm not sure why they treat us so differently. For all they know, I was out partying with friends too.

Honestly, I haven't been talking to anyone after my little spill with Aaron. I'm not mute but I'm afraid that if I talk then something is going to pop out of my mouth that I shouldn't have said. I just had to think about how I exposed my secret to Aaron. I mean, it felt amazing to admit the truth to someone but I was afraid Aaron would tell someone. What would the repercussions be from that? I couldn't risk losing everything me or my family had worked hard for.

After I officially told him, he just sat there and stroked my hair as I blubbered into his shirt. He wrapped his arms around my ribcage and squeezed tighter than

AMY KULP

necessary and on occasions, I could've sworn that he was crying with me. I wasn't sure though since I never looked up at him. I felt his body shake every once in a while too. I didn't know if he felt bad for me or was sad about his uncle.

But if I were Aaron, I would've reacted differently. I wouldn't believe a word I was saying if I had no reason to suspect that my uncle would do that to anyone. Then again, it was the only explanation of why I was so frightened of him. Why would I make up an accusation of someone I didn't even know?

Even the teachers know something is up with me. The classes that I have previously done poorly in were the classes that I was excelling in now. The classes that I was doing amazing in, I was now tanking. Either way, my grades were going to be average now compared to either being excellent or poor. The only reason I've been able to get along with my grades is that my thoughts eventually begin to haunt me or I run out of things to think about. Then I begin to concentrate on the homework that's been given out and that usually lasts me through the night. Even though it gets really dark out here, I never bring light with me. I have my phone light and I'm pretty sure I could take on a wild animal if it tried to attack me. At least yell loud enough for someone to hear me.

Sighing, I picked up my books and stood up. I looked over the guardrail at the busy city and shook my head. I slowly made my way down the hill and stopped when I checked the time.

10:28 P.M.

Checking to see if I have missed any calls or texts, I was amazed as there were none. Usually, mom or dad texted me by now. I smiled as I realized that they finally trusted me to come home by now. Maybe they realized that it was possible for me to have a social life like Luke. Or they just simply forgot about me.

As I walked home, I couldn't help but slow down. There was nothing exciting going on at home and when there was, it wasn't for me to intrude on. Unknown to my parents, I would always sit outside my door for a bit to hear what they were talking about. It was usually about my mom getting interviews for new jobs. I smiled as they continued to talk but hated when the conversation would always turn back to me. About how I was becoming antisocial and then how my dad said I needed counseling.

Or a stern talking to.

That's when I always went back to my room so I didn't need to hear what they thought of me. Honestly, I didn't care what anyone thought of me at the time because I was too worried about Aaron. What happens if he told his uncle and then his uncle convinced him I was lying? What happens if Aaron tells someone? What would happen if he did? Would I be taken away from my family? Would I be shunned at school? I didn't want to think of any of the consequences of what might happen.

Finally getting to my house, I kicked my shoes off lightly and slowly walked up the stairs to hear what my parents were talking about. Hearing my mom's usual jabber, I rolled my eyes and closed my door.

I really needed to shower.

Taking a quick one, I didn't waste time when I got out. I dressed quickly and threw my hair in a sloppy ponytail. I opened my door slowly and leaned my back against the wall to eavesdrop on my parents.

When there was no chatter from downstairs, I slowly made my way down the hallway and peeked my head around to look down at the stairwell. I walked down two steps before sitting down and listening to the complete silence.

I hated complete silence.

By the time I finally heard another noise, I was all the way down the stairs and was startled to catch a glimpse of Luke and a girl standing a bit frightened behind him. I pressed my lips together and walked further. She didn't look like the other girls Luke had dated beforehand. I had to assume that this was the girlfriend I had never met before.

"You should've used protection," I heard my dad whisper. I stopped frozen in my tracks and my eyes grew bigger. "Or you know…" he said more sternly. I knew at any moment he was going to explode with anger. He reacted rougher with Luke and any mistake he made, was ten times worse than if I were to make it.

"You better stay together with this girl," my mom said, a bit shaky but sweetly. "And you better be there for your baby."

I shook my head no and quietly ran up the stairs to

my room. I slammed the door shut and launched my body to my bed. I safely made it and smashed my face into my pillow. I wanted to cry but I knew that I had no real reason to. This baby didn't affect me and if Luke was stupid enough to get one of his side girls pregnant, that was on him. It was just another obstacle to take my brother away from spending some time with me. It's nothing new to me so I'm not even sure why I was worried. I knew that he would do something to get away from me faster and this was just something to practice for. He was eventually going to have a child.

I just didn't think it was for at least five more years.

"Tanner?" Luke asked, opening my door slightly. He sat on my bed and I shifted my body away from him. "Did you hear?" I didn't move to look at him. "I know you were downstairs." I still didn't answer and Luke huffed. "When you want to act mature about this, come find me." I felt him get off of it and stand over me for a second. He expected me to want to talk to him. How could I when he wouldn't even tell me about it? I had to find out through eavesdropping.

As he left the room, I looked up just in time to see that his hair was ruffled up and his eyes were bloodshot. Either he's been crying or he's known for a while and was stressing over how to tell our parents. How to tell anyone.

"Congratulations," I mumbled as he shut the door. As he stomped down the stairs I couldn't help but imagine how her parents were going to take the news. I was surprised that our parents took it so well, although if the girl wasn't around I'm sure Luke would be running out the door in a matter of five seconds. My parents would have reacted differently to the news. Since they had company, they had to control their emotions. My parents would never risk the integrity of their reputation.

I lay back down and drifted to sleep in a matter of seconds. The sleep didn't seem long but as I woke up, I realized that I had overslept to sit at Aaron's spot before school.

Sighing, I got dressed and rushed down the stairs to hurry to school. If I wanted breakfast from school, I had to really run because I had already missed the bus that would take me.

It wasn't a long walk but it was a walk.

As I reared into the school, I basically ran for the door to the entrance. If I had been a minute longer, I would be considered absent from school. I quickly rushed into the lunch room for breakfast and didn't slow down my speed until I have finished and waited for the bell to ring.

"Hey." I stared at Aaron quizzingly as he sat down in front of me. He usually didn't eat breakfast but I was obviously not staring at him for that. He hasn't been to school in a week and he magically shows up today. He barely smiled at me before looking around as if he cared about what other people thought. "Are we still having our tutoring sessions?" he questioned. I nodded my head at him and he just smiled. "Alright, thanks."

And with that, he left me. He dumped his tray without touching a bite of it and with no indication as to where he's been all this week.

He wouldn't even look me in the eyes when he was talking to me. That kind of freaked me out a bit but Aaron probably didn't even know that he was doing it. Maybe he was just trying to be mysterious.

Then again, he's never tried to be before.

I rolled my eyes as I continued the conversation with myself and most likely made facial expressions as I thought with myself. Finally deciding that I should stop thinking to myself, I got up from the table and made my way to my next classes.

I didn't stop to think about what we were learning until I was at the hilltop waiting for Aaron to come. I wasn't exactly sure if he was implying that he was coming but I'm ninety percent sure that he implied it to me when he asked.

Or he was trying to avoid me.

I instantly facepalmed myself since that was probably the reason. He's been avoiding me all week and now he asked if I was still going on the hilltop. No wonder he asked, he wanted to avoid me. He probably didn't want to deal with my emotions and craziness. He didn't want to deal with having to face that his uncle was a child molester.

As I continued to argue with myself in my head, I didn't even hear or process through my mind that someone else was coming up. Mostly because I've been here for weeks and nobody ever comes up here. If it was anyone, I would have assumed it was Aaron.

"Seriously?" I heard someone ask a question. I looked up and was surprised to see my brother at the hill with his girlfriend behind him. "Can I not have anything to myself anymore?" He began stomping away but his girlfriend caught his wrist.

"Just talk to her," the girlfriend whispered. "Besides, she had it first."

Luke seemed stunned for a moment but sat down right beside the girl as she sat down next to me. I honestly didn't want to talk to them at the moment but since they wouldn't leave, I had no choice but to talk back when they attempted a conversation. It was surprising to me that the girl was arguing with him to try and mend our relationship. It was the nicest thing one of his girlfriends have ever done for me.

"Uh, Tanner, this is Marissa." Luke scratched the back of the neck, anticipating my response. I didn't directly snub her but I looked her up and down and turned my head back to look at the view. "Marissa, this is Tanner."

"Right." Marissa tried to be friendly with me but I could tell she was trying too hard to seem like the perfect girlfriend. "Well, I'm sorry that you had to find out about me on the wrong terms."

I shrugged my shoulders at her response and I heard Luke huff. I could tell he was going to say something but he calmed himself when Marissa put her hand on his leg. They passed a look of glances before turning back to me but all I could do was get up and stare out over the view. Marissa joined me at the guardrail while Luke stayed a couple of feet back.

"This is beautiful," she whispered. I nodded my head again and let the wind blow my hair out of the sloppy ponytail I had it in. Marissa looked angelic with her hair blowing in the wind and I couldn't help but feel jealous. Luke always snagged the nice-looking girls. I have never seen him with someone ugly. It made me so self-conscious.

"You guys were dating before you…" I trailed off and hoped that they could catch on to the rest. Marissa obviously did but I caught her glancing at Luke to come forward. When he didn't, she frowned and pursed her lips.

"Luke, go wait in the car," she snarled. "Obviously I'll talk to your sister. Let her lash out at me if she wants without any interruptions." Luke didn't do as she said but once she didn't continue to talk, he went. "Okay, I know that you obviously hate me. I'd hate me too if my brother brought home a pregnant girl." She shook her hair and stared off into the distance. "A girl he wasn't even dating at the time."

I closed my eyes in frustration. Luke was so stupid.

"But it doesn't matter what happened, just now that we're together," she whispered. "But I need you to know, no matter how much you hate me, I'm not going away. Even if Luke and I break up, I'll still be involved because this is both of our babies."

"Alright."

"At least your parents are taking it better than mine," she whispered. I looked at her and she pressed her lips together. "Mine kicked me out of the house and are attempting to get me to give it up for adoption."

"Why aren't you?" I questioned. It wasn't a mean question since I was just curious but most teenage parents would give up for adoption since they still wanted to live their lives.

"Guilt mostly," she whispered.

"So where are you staying?" I wondered. "Because my parents would probably let you sleep in our house. Just not in the same room as Luke."

"Thanks but I'm living with my Aunt for a little while." She shrugged her shoulders at me and then looked out in the city again. "So why were you out here? I saw you come up here so I purposely told Luke about wanting to spend more time together."

"You wanted us to make up?" I questioned. She nodded her head and I thought for a minute. "You're nicer than I thought Marissa." That's all I said before Aaron coming up the hill interrupted us both.

He seemed dazed for a moment since usually, nobody else was up here but he came over to the guard rail like he was part of the group anyway. Marissa looked at me curiously and nodded her head while smiling. She started walking away and smiled suggestively at me.

"I see."

When she disappeared, I stayed frozen in place as Aaron dropped the books on the ground. Aaron sat on the dirt floor expecting me to follow but I stayed standing for a good ten minutes after.

When I eventually did sit down on the floor, we stared at each other. Neither of us spoke but I could tell that Aaron had been thinking the past week and is continuously doing it. Getting uncomfortable, I flipped my English book open and started to read the story that was assigned. Was he caught up in class to be helping and tutoring me at the moment? Should I be tutoring him?

"Did you tell your parents yet?" Aaron asked out of the blue. I looked up at him and finally deduced that we weren't going to do much studying up here. I closed my book and set it aside as I stood up again. I walked to the guardrail and waited until Aaron stood beside me.

"Aaron," I whispered. "If I could take back what I told you, I would." I shook my head at myself and Aaron scooted closer to me.

"I think you should tell them," he whispered.

"It's none of their business."

"It kind of is," he replied. He scooted closer to me and looked at me with caring eyes. "Listen this past week, I've been thinking about it. At first, I didn't want to believe you. I told myself that you were just lying this whole time but then I realized, you don't have a motive as to why you would be lying." Aaron looked out and then sighed. "Honestly, I'm still having my doubts but when you were crying in my car, I had to believe you. Because you were so convincing. It's so hard to believe that my uncle did that to you when he didn't even show a wrong emotion ever."

"Some people are good actors," I mumbled.

"And maybe you are too." Aaron looked at me and when I made eye contact, he shifted away first. "But the way you act when we talk about him..." He nodded his head and shivered. "Please tell your parents, Tanner." I didn't say anything as Aaron pushed me further. "Don't you want justice for what he did?"

"No," I whispered. I nodded my head no and looked Aaron dead in the eye. "I don't want justice, I want him to get out of my life." I felt tears welled up in my eyes. "Just let it go, Aaron." I started walking away from him but when he spoke, it made my whole body shiver and shake.

"But what happens if he did it to others?" I froze in place and slowly turned to look at Aaron. My lip quivered as he continued to stare at me and I shook my head. I looked towards the ground and started walking away but against Aaron's protests, I could still hear him. "Fine, Tanner. You win for now! But we're not done discussing this!"

I didn't want to win though. Secretly I wanted him to tell my parents but I don't think they would believe me. Nobody would believe me. Even Aaron said he didn't believe me when I told him. Why would anybody else believe me? Especially after one year has passed since the incidents. Nobody would believe me.

Plus, it's really bad timing.

With Luke's girlfriend being pregnant, it would just seem like I'm trying to outdo them. Like I wanted to be the center of attention so I made a whole scheme to have them out of the spotlight and on the sideline. That's the way Luke would see it too. Since Luke and I are somewhat in a fight, he would just think everything is bad and would think I'm doing this on purpose.

But as I continued to walk towards my house, my mind drifted towards what Aaron said.

What would happen if he did it to other girls? If he did it to multiple girls, at least one of them would've told someone. He wouldn't have a teaching job and no school would ever hire him ever again so it was impossible that he did it to other girls.

Unless they were like me.

I was so alone at that school. I didn't have any friends and I know that I kept to myself. My parents were often stressed and having the extra credit opportunities made them even more stressed. I was usually an A student and seeing as they thought I was slipping, put more stress on them that they weren't parenting me right. After convincing them that they were doing the best any parent could do, I took the extra credit opportunities. I just didn't tell my parents what went on in the sessions.

Of course, the extra credit sessions were probably fake. I was probably doing very well in the class the whole time but I was too naïve to see through it all.

Besides, it's my fault it happened anyway. After

the first time, I shouldn't have gone back. I just placed myself in the situation even further and I should've known that my instincts of being uncomfortable were right.

"Tanner?" Aaron asked as he drove by me. I kept my head to the ground and walked on forward. He pulled his car as close to the sidewalk as he could and matched my speed. It didn't matter if he followed me all of the way home though. A five-minute difference was not going to want to make me talk to him about it. I'm not sure how he thought it would. "You have to tell someone about what he did to you." I shook my head and continued walking. I was trying to ignore him, but I know that I couldn't. I liked being around him and I didn't want all of our interactions to be terrible with each other. "Maybe there are other girls who want to see him brought to justice but are too frightened."

"What about me, Aaron?" I questioned harshly. I turned to him and stared at Aaron through the car windows. "What about how I feel?" Aaron seemed puzzled for a moment and then pulled up. "I can't even look at him without trembling anymore! I'm afraid of him, Aaron! Why do you think I've never told anyone before? Why do you think I want to take back that night when I told you? It's better to be a secret because when it was a secret, I didn't have to deal with whether or not you were going to do something!" I stared at Aaron and he seemed shocked too.

Finally, he cracked a smile under the pressure and

managed to chuckle softly.

"I never thought I'd see the day when you admit that you're frightened." He chuckled some more and shook his head. Honestly, I couldn't help but crack a tiny smile too because Aaron always knew how to look on the bright side. Even in impossible situations.

Of course, I didn't necessarily smile at what he said next.

"But Tanner, if you don't tell your parents, I will."

Chapter Sixteen

Honestly, I thought Aaron was lying when he said that he would tell my parents. It's been a week since we've talked about it and he has yet to tell anyone. There weren't any rumors going around school about me. I was still being treated normally as well. The only change in friendship I have is with Aaron. Since he's threatened me, we have stopped talking altogether. He hasn't been attending our tutoring sessions nor has he come up on the hill. Since I no longer box, I haven't seen him in the gym either. Secretly, I hope every day he will talk to me or show up to tutor me. Despite how upset I was with him, my grades mattered to me. Whenever he didn't show up, I would work on the homework anyway. While my grades weren't as good when I was with him, they were better than before.

He also mattered to me. I didn't want my secret being the reason we weren't friends. I didn't want it to ruin our friendship. This secret has ruined so much for me and I didn't want Aaron to be one of them. He was the best part of this last move for me.

That's why I was completely surprised when I came home to a dimmed house. Now that my mom was jobless, she usually greeted me in the doorway and had all of the lights on in the house. While we were being warned to keep our electricity bill low, my mom must have been exempt during the day. However, there was only one light on when I came to my house. I kicked my shoes off and put my backpack down before following the light to the kitchen.

The first person I saw was Luke. He was sitting on the floor against our cupboards. His head was down between his legs and he had his hands clasped together. He looked like he was mourning the loss of something. Maybe it was the loss of his free time or the loss of his playboy ways. I stood silently for a moment to look at him but he didn't register that I was there. He didn't look up at me and kept his head down. While odd, it wasn't as odd as when I heard sniffles.

I turned around to see Aaron sitting at my dinner table. He was joined by my mom and my dad. My dad's face was extremely red and his jaw was tightened. If I saw him on the side of the street, I would assume he just got done exercising. He held onto my mom as she cried into his shirt. She was wailing and the main reason nobody had heard me come in. When my eyes roamed back to Aaron, he had a saddened expression on his face. I think he was the only one who knew that I was in the room. While his head was turned in my general direction, he refused to make eye contact with me.

I shook my head at him because I knew. I knew he had told everybody about me. He betrayed me and told my family. He told my family the biggest secret I have ever kept from them. He had told them something I wanted to stay a secret. I made a mistake trusting him with it.

The tears threatening to spill down my cheeks forced me to run out of the room. They would soon notice me and start treating me differently. Start treating me like I was a child. Start treating me like I couldn't take care of myself. I left the house without putting my shoes on and sprinted. I wasn't sure where I was running to but I let my legs carry me. When they carried me up the familiar hill, I smiled at the familiarity.

I didn't stop until I reached the spot on the hilltop. I leaned against the guardrail and let myself cry. It was such good therapy for me right now and I just slumped my whole body until the guardrail was the only thing that was keeping me up. I would've been lying on the ground if it wasn't there. I let myself cry like I never have before. I involved my throat and allowed myself to make noise. While I was ashamed to admit it, it felt like such a relief to permit myself to do this.

"Tanner…" Aaron said as I heard leaves crunch beneath his feet. He had run up this hill but now that he was on top and saw me in a broken state, he walked slowly and carefully towards me. "I'm sorry but it had to be done."

"No, it didn't," I rejected. I shook my head as I wiped my face with my dirty jacket. I cried harder when I heard him step closer. "You don't even know what you did now." I sniffled the snot that was coming out of my nose and felt Aaron's presence behind me. "Leave me alone, Aaron." Aaron placed a hand on my back but I shook it off. I managed to look at him through my teary eyes and saw the sadness on his face. "Don't talk to me ever again. I don't even want to see you." Aaron seemed hurt but he didn't bother leaving. "Leave."

"You don't mean that, Tanner." He sounded so unsure that when he said it, I thought it was a question. I nodded my head and wiped at my eyes again.

"You don't understand, Aaron. You weren't the one being manipulated!" I yelled. He seemed taken back at my yelling and as I continued to cry, I watched as he shook his head and slowly walked behind him. He was slowly retreating to his house and I couldn't help but feel the pain of guilt. It soon vanished when I remembered my mom crying, my dad about to cry, and Luke in that vulnerable ball position.

What would my mom think of me now? She would never be able to trust me because of what she knows. She'll treat me like a kid forever and would be wondering where I was every hour of the day. She'll start being a parent and that was so scary to me..

My dad. He would never be able to look at me again without feeling some sort of guilt. But after all of this time, he'll finally know why I stopped trying to talk to him and every other male species on the earth of this planet. They'll finally realize why I am the way I am.

Luke. He's going to hate me. I know for a fact that he'll attempt to pull the "she's just trying to outdo me" card. He'll think I'm trying to be the center of attention again but in reality, I just want to be the cameo role. I hate attention which is why I've never told anyone.

Plus I was dead frightened to tell anyone.

As time passed on, I slowly regained my composure and finally managed to sit up straight. I looked out in the darkness and knew that I wouldn't be going home tonight. It was already three in the morning and it was a weekend.

I could just run away and my parents would never know. Then again, I knew that I couldn't run away. I was too dependent on a bed and school to do much of anything on my own. If I lived out in the wild, I'd be the first dead because I accidentally ate poisonous berries.

Realizing that I did need to go home, I let the soil sink between my toes and squished my way home. As I stepped onto the porch, I breathed out before actually taking hold of the door handle and walking in. The house was still dark and I was thankful for that because I made my way up to my room with ease.

Grabbing my clothes, I went into the bathroom and took a quick shower. As I got dressed, I couldn't help but stare in the mirror at my body. There were no lasting marks and there was no video proof, so even if I wanted to testify I wouldn't be able to do it.

There was just my opinion on the stand. And I'm certain that they would bring up Tanner's death as a way of me wanting more attention or something like that. Honestly, I just want it to all blow over so that I could return to being a normal girl.

As I stepped into my room and hopped into my bed, I soon realized that I would never be a normal teenage girl. My thoughts haunted me. Any memory would haunt me.

I will always be haunted at what happened those days but there was no way I could take any of that back. There was no way to erase my mind. There wasn't even a way I could get payback for him because if I did try to take him down in court, he would bring up false accusers like his nephew.

Who did I have on my side? Aaron and that's all. He wasn't even there so it couldn't even be possible to have him testify with me.

Slowly as I continued to think about this, I soon became rather drowsy and wished to fall asleep right on the spot. But I couldn't because soon my door was opened wearily and my parents entered my room.

I guess they thought I was asleep because my mom sat on my bed and sniffled a bit. She started petting my head but it was just uncomfortable for all of us.

"Do you think he was telling us the truth?" she questioned. My father sat down on the bed and I could feel his eyes on me too.

"Nobody would lie about that." He shifted his weight on the bed and I closed my eyes tightly. "And if they do…" I could tell that my dad was shaking his head because he always did when he trailed off. "We should leave her tonight though. We'll talk to her about it tomorrow."

AMY KULP

"Is that the right move though?" my mom asked me. "Maybe she didn't tell us for a specific reason. I don't think we should testify unless she wants to."

"You want this man to walk free?" my dad asked semi-angry. I could tell they were going to start yelling so I shifted my body a little and they both shut up for a bit. "Let's just leave her and we'll discuss this tomorrow."

My mom hugged my still body and left the room. I started to relax in my bed until I felt my dad come near me and kiss me on the head. Once he left, I opened my eyes but stayed in the still position that I was in.

I'm surprised that my mom was going to take my side. Usually, she would want justice and I was silently thinking my dad would make her. My mom might be threatening but my dad was an incredible person when he wanted to be convincing.

I sighed though.

Why did my parents have to find out the hard way? If I had told them, they wouldn't have believed me and that would've been better. But it kind of hurt that they believed a stranger over me. Then again, I would never know if they would believe me because I didn't get a chance to say anything.

Not that I was going to anyway.

Chapter Seventeen

As I looked at the view from my seat on the dirty ground, I couldn't help but hear someone come up the hill. I didn't mind much since only three people knew about it. Since Aaron and I haven't been talking, it was either Luke or his girlfriend. I didn't think it was his girlfriend since she didn't have a reason to talk to me right now. None of this had to do with her and I was hoping that Luke would leave her out of this. I didn't want a lot of people to know and I was worried she would spread the gossip around the school. I didn't want to be pitied.

As he came and sat down next to me, I kept staring off. There was no need to acknowledge him right now. He stared at the view as well. When we became more comfortable with each other, I started synchronizing my breathing with his. Once in a while, I would hear a small hiccup in his breath so I knew that he was withholding a cry. I didn't want his sympathy. I didn't want pity.

I'm not sure if he heard my argument this morning with mom and dad. He was probably still asleep but with how loud we had gotten, I wouldn't be surprised if he had woken up. They started by just staring at me until I got too uncomfortable. My dad questioned why I had never told anyone and I just shrugged my shoulders. They wanted real answers to everything they were asking.

Every time they raised their voice, I shifted my gaze to their feet. I didn't want to be guilted for not telling them. My mom cursed under her breath a bit and then asked if I wanted to testify. When I looked up, I could see my parents giving each other glares and my face ended up screwing up before I said no. I bit my lip and waited for a reaction but my mom just kept staring at me. I could tell she wanted me to say yes but I dropped my gaze back down before I could change my mind. We sat in silence for two straight hours afterward. They were hoping that they could pressure me into testifying. It eventually ended because my dad had to go to work and I had to go to school.

I've been sitting out here for a couple of hours but it wasn't as tense as when I was with my parents. They just kept staring me down and I couldn't help but feel guilty that I didn't tell them. My mom looked so hurt when she looked at me but when I wasn't looking, she would just stare at me. It looked like she was pondering a question to ask me but never had enough courage to go through with it and ask me. My dad didn't show any emotion though. It wasn't that hard to believe because my dad never showed emotion. He was a stone-cold statue.

"I think you should testify," Luke finally said. I looked at him a little confused and when he looked up, I knew he meant what he said. "It can't hurt to try." He shrugged his shoulders and picked at the grass. "The worst thing that could happen is you lose."

I faced the sky again and steadied my breath away from his. He scooted closer to me and without my knowledge, hugged me. It wasn't a simple two-second hug either because it lasted longer than it should have. I didn't break away from it though because I was confused.

Luke was supposed to be angry with me. He was supposed to yell at me for making accusations against something that never happened and then say I was just doing it to overshadow him. Instead, this caring demeanor was left in place of my brother and I couldn't help but wonder if he was pretending or not.

Once he let go, he looked at me with his brown eyes and then sighed himself. He looked back out at the view and I heard him part his lips.

"Did you even try to stop it?" he questioned. I nodded my head, yes and the grunt that Luke produced was much worse than the other one. "I'm sorry I wasn't there."

"It's fine," I whispered.

"It really isn't," he whispered. "Is it my fault that this happened?" I looked at him questioningly and he gulped before he looked straight at me. "You asked me that one time to come with you but I went with my girlfriend instead. Then I saw the hickies on your neck and I never said anything. Then I started teasing you about them and…" Luke shook his head and ruffled his hair. "Why didn't you tell me, Tanner?" His voice got all squeaky and it rose high as tears started forming in the corner of his eyes. "I just thought you had a boyfriend! I didn't think that you were…" He shook his head in disgust and I saw a teardrop drip down his face. "It's all my fault, isn't it?" he questioned. "I should've known something was wrong and came with you that day." He shook his head again. "Why didn't you tell anyone Tanner?" As more tears appeared running down his cheeks, he turned to me and only then did I realize that he expected me to answer him.

"He told… me not to."

"Why did you listen to him, Tanner? Why did you keep going to those extra credit opportunities? Why did you put yourself through this torture?"

"I couldn't stop it, Luke." I licked my lips and felt Luke's gaze land on me. "You don't know what went on during those sessions. He acted like nothing happened for months and then I slowly forgave him. Then he would do it again and…" I shook my head and shrugged my shoulders. "We moved and I thought I would never see him again."

"What do you mean you thought?" he questioned. I shrugged my shoulders but when he hit me in the back of the head, I knew he knew I was lying.

"He moved in the neighborhood." I shrugged my shoulders and I saw Luke's jaw tighten. "He moved to help Aaron and his mom with the electricity."

"Wait, wasn't Aaron the one who told mom and dad about the incident?" Luke asked, trailing off. I nodded my head and he see stumped for a moment. "Is he still living with him?"

"I have no clue," I whispered. "But even if he is, he needs to be because Aaron and his mom need that house or they're downsizing."

"I don't care, Tanner. We have to get him out of that house." Luke instantly got up and waited for me to follow. When I didn't, he pulled me along and eventually ended up dragging me along the dirt path. "Come on. I don't care if you guys are in a fight, he did the right thing."

Once we got in the car, I gave the directions to his house and stayed still in Luke's car as he got Aaron. When they finally came out, Luke was basically dragging along Aaron and his fist was stained in a blood-red. I gasped when I realized what that meant but didn't have time to comprehend it because Aaron was thrown in the back and Luke gunned the gas.

"This is considered kidnapping, you know," Aaron protested. Luke shrugged and wiped the blood on his pants so that nobody would see it. "Besides, he's never done anything to me, just her."

I gave Aaron a face before returning to my thoughts. From what I'm guessing was that Luke punched Craig in the face or somewhere else. I felt myself smile at the thought but snapped myself out of it when we parked the car at our house.

When we got in the house, Aaron crossed his arms and stared at me hard. I looked back at him but broke the gaze away from him in a couple of minutes. Aaron looked confused for a moment and then looked towards Luke.

"Is she testifying?" he questioned.

Luke looked towards me and I nodded my head no. Luke grunted at me and stomped his way up the stairs. When I heard the door slam behind him, I excused myself for my room.

After a few minutes alone, I let Aaron into my room since I knew he followed me up. He walked in and I slowly closed the door. When I got comfortable, I let Aaron look around my room and he sighed.

"Just testify," Aaron whispered. "I can't stand to look at my Uncle anymore."

I nodded my head no but honestly, I wasn't so sure anymore. I had Luke to testify with me, Craig's nephew, and Aaron could too. I also could use my journal I wrote in once and a while because that was the only thing that could keep me sane for a while.

"I'll be there whether and I'll be on your side." Before Aaron could leave, he stared at me intently and then spoke again. "And your family will support you no matter what."

"You don't know that."

"Tanner, they were crying when they found out. Your mom was hysterical and your dad started crying when you ran out. Luke couldn't even show his face because he was crying."

"My dad was crying?" I asked. Aaron nodded his head and then he left for upstairs.

Honestly, my dad doesn't show much emotion. He barely even smiled. So it was concerning that my dad would cry, I felt like it would suit him more if his jaw clenched and he wanted to punch something. It frightened me more than anything else to know that my dad cried over something simply because my dad was that tall, plump dad with a beer gut. He was the dad that all of your friends were afraid of when you were eight, and some still are.

Getting out of my room, I knocked on Luke's door before going in. He was laying on his bed with the computer on his lap and I could tell he was either looking something up or video chatting with someone. I sat at the edge of his bed without saying anything until finally, he looked at me.

"Were you crying?" I questioned. He seemed a bit confused as to what I meant so he placed his computer on his desk and sat up with me. "When you found out, were you crying?" Luke nodded his head but pressed his lips in a firm line. "Was dad?"

It took a moment before Luke replied to me. "Yes."

At that moment, I felt my world crumble down. My eyebrows weakened to the center point, my lips were turned down at the end, and my eyes were squinting back tears. Instantly, Luke brought me into a hug and managed to hear Luke whisper, even though it wasn't directed towards me.

"You know, I've never seen you or dad cry…" He paused for a moment. "And it breaks my heart seeing it happen in the same week." I clutched onto Luke's shirt and he patted my head uneasily. "Because I never in my life would've imagined you going through something like this. I always pictured you as a warrior." I sniffled and attempted to steady my breath but couldn't help but have it falter. "I never thought you were breakable."

"Luke..." I let go of Luke and stared up with puppy dog eyes. "I changed my mind, I-I want to testify."

Chapter Eighteen

"Is this the place?" Aaron asked as he pulled his car up to the building. I looked over to see if it looked familiar to the pictures I have seen on the internet. It didn't. I shrugged my shoulders and looked nervously at the front steps. Beeps from other cars forced me out of my anxious state and had me reaching for the door handle. "Let me find where to park first." He pulled forward and started surrounding the building until he came across an adjacent parking lot. While we weren't sure it belonged to them, Aaron would remain in the car so he could easily move it if needed. "Are you sure you want to go in alone?" he asked. I nodded my head but felt butterflies in the pit of my stomach.

"I lied," I whispered. I closed my eyes and tried to breathe in a pattern - in and out, in and out, in and out. "I don't think I want to do this." My clutch on the armrests tightencd and instinctively reached for my missing necklace. I haven't worn it in months but I was still grabbing at it when I was nervous.

"Your appointment isn't for fifteen more minutes." He turned the music off and I heard him adjust how he was sitting. I popped open one eye to see him staring at me. "Let's distract you until then." He grabbed at one of my hands to stop me from twiddling them and I turned to look at him. "Why did you ask me to come with you today? Why not someone from your family?" I closed my eyes and felt myself beginning to blush. "You are going to need to be okay with answering uncomfortable questions, Tanner. Are you still going through with the trial?" I nodded my head and opened them slightly. When I realized he wasn't going to taunt me, I opened them the rest of the way.

"You know how hard it is for me to open up emotionally." I kept my voice low and I could see that he was straining to hear me. "I don't want my family knowing that I need to... *talk* about my feelings."

"That's normal, Tanner." I shook my head to protect but he didn't let me open my mouth before he interjected. "You went through *trauma*. You need a safe place to go and get help. What you are going to go through for the next couple of months may unleash things that you or I may not understand. You need to work through these things."

I nodded my head in agreement and swallowed the lump in my throat. I wanted to argue but knew there was no point. Aaron and I were raised in two different environments. Aaron was someone who was willing to help anyone who needed it. He had a safe environment to talk about his feelings. I didn't like to help anyone besides myself and I grew up in an environment that thought it was weird to get emotional.

"I'm going to..." I trailed off and Aaron just nodded his head for me to go.

As I walked out of his car, I felt the sickness in my stomach again. I breathed out once before I started walking towards the building. It was a short distance and the road that I had to cross was not busy. I could do this.

The building itself did not look like the building from the pictures I have seen. I forced Aaron to GPS it though so I knew that this was the address. I couldn't see a sign that said the place that it was but it made sense that I wouldn't. This was a secretive organization. It was for the protection of myself and others.

As I opened the door, I grew embarrassed when the doors were too heavy for me to pull. Thankfully when I arrived, almost nobody was in the room. I looked around and saw an extremely white room - the flooring, the walls, the doors, the desk, everything. I could hear my echo as I started walking down it and noticed the different names on the door. When I couldn't find the one I wanted, I walked up to the only girl at her desk.

"I'm looking for the..." I mumbled. The girl looked at me as if I spoke another language. I looked around the room and felt my mouth go dry. "The victim's center."

"Oh!" She giggled to herself as if it was a joke between us but soon remained her professional demeanor. "That's downstairs. Take those stairs and you are all set."

I nodded my head and smiled at her as I walked down there. I immediately felt more sickness in my stomach and realized that I was making myself physically ill from how nervous I was. As soon as I stepped my foot on the last step, I saw a bathroom door ajar and rushed inside.

I locked the door immediately and felt myself drop to my knees. Could I do this? I felt like I had to throw up. I forced myself to hover over the toilet for a couple of minutes before I got up. I stared at myself in the mirror and splashed cool water on my face. That would help, right? When I dried it off, I looked at my reflection before nodding my head at myself and telling myself to go.

The basement was very odd. There wasn't any noise that I could hear and there were not that many doors to choose from. I went to my right but was only met with closed doors. They wouldn't all be closed doors, right? I wandered over to my left and found an open floor of little offices. I sheepishly grabbed at my purse as I entered the room. Everybody was busy on their phones or computers. Do I interrupt them?

"How may I help you?" one lady asked as she hung up the phone. She seemed cheery and I thought it felt odd in this quiet place. I stepped closer to her and looked around to make sure nobody else was listening. She kept a smile on her face despite me being skeptical.

"I have an appointment," I whispered. "For Tan-Chloe. Chloe." I looked nervously around the room again and she happily clicked on her computer. She nodded her head and looked at her phone when it began to ring again.

"Just take a seat in the room to your right."

I nodded my head and immediately walked to my right. It was a small little room that she had me in. There were only five chairs to sit in - two clustered together and then a set of three. I chose to sit in the middle of the three-seater so that I was able to look at the door. The chairs were not comfortable at all. The armrests were a bit too high and the cushions were too new to give any comfort. As I surveyed the rest of the room, I was able to get a better picture of what this place was.

There were tons of pamphlets across the wall and scattered across every surface. There were some for stalking, fire, pregnancy, robbery, assault, comfort, counseling, and others. I scanned them quickly and was too afraid that someone would see me touch one if I tried to grab it. In the corner of the room was a TV that was off. Below it was a VCR tape collection of movies that someone could watch. Was I too old to watch a movie? As my gaze dropped to the floor, I noticed all of the discarded toys around the room. They were disorganized and thrown all about so it was clear that they were recently played with.

What a sad thought.

The last thing for me to notice was the red phone near the TV. There was a sign plastered above it saying to call it if you didn't get serviced within five minutes. I blushed at the thought. Was I supposed to go in here before talking to that lady? Did I interrupt her? At the thought, I felt myself beginning to chew the inside of my cheek.

I wish I had brought my phone in. At least then I would be able to distract myself from the pit in my stomach. It was only getting worse as I waited longer. It had to be past my scheduled time right? Were these people usually punctual? Or were they late?

"I'm sorry, I needed to ask you a couple more questions." The lady came forward and sat next to me. She had a clipboard with paper and I felt intimidated. I hope they didn't need my personal information. I didn't want anyone to know that I was here. "You have been using our hotline right?" I nodded my head. "You have been chatting with Ms. Gadio, correct?" I nodded my head but interrupted her before she could ask me anything else.

"Can I have someone else?" She scrunched her eyebrows down her face as she has never been asked that before. "I don't feel as though she is right for me." I gulped and looked around the room. I haven't seen anybody besides this lady. Would I be okay to confide in her? "She kept blaming me for putting myself in the situation." Did this lady even know my situation? I was tired of having to repeat it so much.

"I see." She nodded her head and put her pen on the paper. She excused herself again and I found my voice going shaky.

Breathe in.

Breathe out.

Now that she was gone, I could relax at the thought of having a new counselor. I closed my eyes and while I was unnerved by how long this process was, it felt relaxing to know that I would be getting all of these thoughts out of my system. Somebody could help me and figure out why I feel like I am feeling. These people know how to help me.

I just didn't want to think of myself as a victim.

***

My body ached.

    My lips were bruised.

    My neck was sore.

    My pulse was uneven.

    My mind was numb.

    My feet shuffled down the hallways as I clutched harder onto my bag strap. It was slung over my shoulder and I felt every time that it whacked my back. I wanted to scream out but my body was already buzzing. As I walked past my lockers, I stopped short when I saw the guidance counselors' office. I turned my body and looked in.

    Their office was partitioned off from the hallway. While I could see inside from the glass windows, I was not able to hear what they were saying. Maybe I could tell one of them? I stepped towards their offices but immediately felt a tug at my arm.

    My body was too sore to protest so as it was thrashed around, I winced at every move. I closed my eyes until I stopped spinning and sat on my bottom. I shoved a whimper down my throat so I wouldn't make a noise as I felt my presence was not wanted. I opened my eyes and saw the nephew here.

"Let me see it." He crossed his arms and held out his hand expectantly. I blinked at him as I tried to process what he wanted. He hasn't said anything to me since he caught his uncle with me. "I know that today is your last day of school." He paused and I blinked at him again. "I also know that you needed to get your final grades." I nodded my head and carefully reached out of my pocket. He angrily ripped it open and read it.

I'm not sure how he knew that Luke and I needed our grades. He probably saw Luke grabbing his final grades from every teacher. Of course, I had to do the same thing. Of course, I had to get my final grades from his Uncle.

Where he gave me a lasting impression.

"You must be joking?" he asked. I snapped out of my thoughts and carelessly made eye contact with him. He shoved my report in my face and angrily threw it to the ground. "You claim to be a victim when you were trading for services?" he asked. I squinted at him and he shoved both of his arms into my shoulders. I winced as the force made me fall over even more and he got on top of me. "You are pathetic and a liar!" I must not have reacted how he wanted me to because he kicked me in the leg. "What's wrong with you?" He kicked me again before freezing. His eyes grew wide and he looked down at me. "Are you on your period?"

I didn't answer and remained still. I wish he would just leave already. My body was sore enough. He didn't though. He remained there and looked at me in horror.

"Are you on your period?"

I shook my head and looked at what made him repeat his question. When I looked, I saw that my jeans had a bloodstain on them. It was slowly leaking and growing bigger. I immediately tied the jacket I had around my waist and tugged so that it would cover the stain. People would just assume that I was on my period. They wouldn't know the real reason.

Craig Moore.

"Get up." His nephew forced me up and immediately straightened me out. He didn't say anything else as he walked me back out to the hallway. I lost track of him as he dodged his way through the student body. As I stared off, Luke came shimmying up to me in no time.

"Hey, you ready to go?" I looked over at the guidance counselors' office to see that the rooms were already black. They were already gone. "Our final day in school, how was it?" he asked as he started walking ahead of me. I didn't say anything as he said bye to some of his classmates. I didn't say anything as we entered his car. "How'd you do on your final grades?"

"Got all A's."

***

AMY KULP

"This is going to be a very long and hard process," Michelle mentioned. I stared at her as I listened to the static machine near the door. It helped ensure that nobody could hear what we were talking about if they walked by the door. I wasn't sure if it worked but it made me feel better. I nodded my head to show her I understood. "There will be times you will absolutely hate me." I smirked a bit but quickly shook it off my face and nodded my head. "But I will always be here for you."

"I haven't made the initial report," I whispered. She leaned towards me and it took her a moment to process what I said. She immediately jotted it down and opened up her planner.

"We can schedule a visit to the police station as soon as you want to." She wrote in the planner and I smiled at her.

Michelle was very direct. It was a little offputting when she first introduced herself to me but now I like her. She isn't going to skirt around any ideas for the sake of me. While she is here to help me through my problems, she is also here to make sure I am represented. To make sure my voice was heard. I was surprised that I found someone I like so fast though. Michelle was mad and allowed me to be angry too.

She understood me.

"Now something that the police will want is evidence." She paused for a moment and I shook my head. I didn't have any. "What did you do with those pants that you had?"

"I left them at that house."

I felt my voice crack and immediately wanted to cry. Did I just mess this whole thing up by doing that? My eyebrows furrowed and my forehead had my usual wrinkles in it. She quickly wrote something down on her notepad and placed her hand on me.

"Do not be upset by that." She shrugged her shoulders. "That's a normal reaction to want to get rid of the evidence." She smiled gently at me but I still felt upset by it. "Did you get a rape kit done at all?"

"No," I warned. My voice grew heavy with her and I felt my instinct to bolt. I had to stop myself from getting up and leaving. "I wasn't raped."

The look of pity that Michelle gave me infuriated me. Who was she to tell me what happened? I just told her my life story so that she would get caught up. I could have left details out or not said any of them. She didn't know me like I knew what happened. She needed to trust me. I was not raped.

I was still a virgin.

"Chloe, you need to calm down," Michelle cooed. I nodded my head and darted my eyes around the room. "It's okay to cry." I continued looking at the ceiling as she said more soothing things to me. They weren't working. Why wasn't it working? She handed me a tissue and I felt the tears beginning to overflow. "I did not mean to upset you."

"I wasn't raped," I repeated. She nodded her head and sat there as I tried to stop the tears. She didn't say anything else until the tears stopped flowing.

"Chloe, part of my job is to help those who need counseling." She paused and looked through her pad of paper. "Part of my job is to help people come to terms with what happened." I shook my head in protest. "You just told me about the bloody pants, right?" she asked. She lowered her voice so that I wouldn't startle and I breathed out. I nodded my head, I didn't want to think about it again. "If you don't mind sharing with me, what caused the bleeding?"

It felt like my words got caught in my throat. While I opened my mouth to talk, no noise came out. My mind was frozen and it was like I couldn't talk. I nudged the tissue under my nose to wipe away any excess snot that was sneaking out. I felt the tears forming again and let them roll down my cheeks effortlessly. There was no resistance as I struggled to say any of the words. I stared at the ceiling so I couldn't see her disappointed look in me I just couldn't bring myself to say it.

I shuddered at the memory.

I shuddered as I remember going into his room right before the bell rang. I was happy. I thought all of the torture that I have experienced with him was finally going to be over. I swaggered into that room like I owned it. My cockiness was radiating off of me and it probably pissed him off. There was no way he planned that ahead of time. It was a spur of the moment decision. I still don't know what prompted him. It seemed that once I got distracted with my final grades, he found the perfect opportunity to give me a lasting impression. He took what I had in my hands, tore my jeans and underwear down my thighs, and when I bent to grab them, he shoved it into me.

I remember the pain.

I remember the humiliation.

I remember tripping over my pantlegs trying to pull them up. He was able to shove it farther in. I remember yelling.

I don't remember how I left the situation.

I don't remember much else.

I only remember how much it had hurt.

I only remember being grateful that he chose to harm me with the eraser side and not the point side of the pencil.

I instantly bent down at the thought and vomited on the carpet. As soon as it left my mouth, I was embarrassed. There was tears coming from my eyes, snot coming from my nose, and vomit coming from my mouth. I instantly wiped at all three as Michelle handed me more tissues. She didn't look repulsed that I threw up in her carpet. She didn't look at me with pity either. She just nodded her head and stood up.

"We don't need to uncover that memory yet, okay?" she asked. I nodded my head vigorously and she motioned for me to get up. I carefully stepped around the carpet and she gently tugged at my wrist. I followed her around to different rooms until we found an identical one we were in.

Once in, she let me sit down as she left the room. Probably was going to tell someone to clean it. Or maybe she was going to clean it herself. I blushed red and let my tongue glide over my teeth as I felt embarrassed by my actions. Why did I react like that? The taste from the vomit wasn't leaving my mouth and I felt repulsed again. I forced myself to stop before I would vomit in this clean room as well.

When she returned, her sternness was back in her posture but her face remained delicate. I couldn't tell what her ploy was now or if she wanted to talk anymore. Did I decide that or her? I gulped as she jotted notes in her book and felt my tongue becoming dry.

While I was still nervous to be around her, I liked that. It was easier to tell a complete stranger about what had happened than my own family. Than people I knew. She didn't have a reason to not believe me and she didn't have a motive behind her curiosity. She only wanted to know more about it so she knew how to handle the situation with me. So she could understand why I was so angry.

I couldn't imagine having her job. Imagine having her job where you hear people complain all day. Sometimes people complain just to complain. She had to try and find solutions to help them. I'm sure that it was draining to hear people complaining all day. How was she so positive? Did she have a family? Was her job her life?

"Stop analyzing me, Chloe," she said as she jotted her final notes. She looked up at me and smiled. "Did you want to plan a different day for a session? You seem to have paused in admitting things to me." I nodded my head and she looked at her calendar. I agreed to the date she gave and I smiled.

"I want to plan my visit to the police station." I bit my bottom lip and looked at her as her eyes widened. I already felt better by talking to her. Imagine what I would feel like once he was behind bars. "You have to be there though."

"Do you know your way out?" she asked. "It was nice meeting you. I wish it was under better circumstances."

I shot back a small smile and exited the room. I quickly made my way up the stairs and when I got outside, I smiled as I saw Aaron's head leaning against the window. He looked like he was sleeping but I couldn't be sure.

"How was it?" he asked as I climbed into the car. I looked at him and his smile changed. "You look terrible."

I nodded my head and buckled up. I was exhausted and I knew it was from the mental exercise. All of the things that I have hidden deep down. All of the things that I never admitted to anyone. They have all finally come up. It was exhausting.

"I just want to go home."

***

AMY KULP

"He needs to go back to sensitivity training!"

Michelle was on a tirade. She was angrier than I was and for once, I was finally able to see what I looked like to other people. Did I look this insane to other people? I stood by her side though because I liked the fire that she had. It made me feel like she cared about me. She shook her head as she left the building and we got into her care. Her face was set in stone and if I were to slide a paper against her chin, she would cut right through it. She waited until I put my seatbelt on before she dialed a number on her phone and waited impatiently for the other side to pick up. I immediately tuned them out when she began roughly speaking with them.

Today was the day that I officially gave my statement to the police. The man that I had gotten was rough. He wasn't gentle when he talked to me and it frightened me when I gave my report. I verbally told him what had happened and he would ask me questions as if he didn't believe me. There were some answers I could not give. I either couldn't remember the answers or my memory had blocked it from me. I was also nervous so I misspoke a little bit. He didn't like when I corrected myself either. Once I was done with my verbal report, I had to write down what had happened. He sat there the whole time and stared at me. I felt very rushed and like I was being judged. While Michelle was with me, she was not allowed to talk to me. She could only shoot glares towards him and sympathetic faces to me.

I wish she was able to talk. I wasn't sure if I was reacting normally and I needed her to tell me. I needed her to let me know if I was being rational. She couldn't tell me that though. So every time he interrupted my story and asked me a question, I lost track of what I was saying. I would try to focus on what I was saying but the moment got lost. I was frustrated and I wanted to cry. Why couldn't he wait to ask his questions?

She continued arguing over the phone to her management and giving out information on the police officer who took our report. I was afraid that her acting this way would harm my report though. What if it got back to him so he wrote that I was lying? Were they able to put their own opinions in their reports?

"I am so sorry about that, Chloe." She shook her head as she ended the call. She put her phone in her purse and began driving us back to the center. I didn't say anything as she drove. I felt like it wasn't as secure as to when we were in her office "You were very brave," she mentioned when she parked her car. I nodded my head and we quickly made our way down to the center. When we were securely in one of the room and she put the static machine on, I felt myself relax. "How do you feel?"

"Scared," I admitted. "What should I expect now?"

"You're going to need to wait." She paused and thought to herself before repeating it out loud. "We are going to continue our sessions so that they can't manipulate you when you are on the stand. You need to get yourself a lawyer though."

I nodded my head. My mom has been working on getting a lawyer for me. I don't know how far she has gotten but I knew that it would cost them a pretty penny. What if we couldn't afford one?

"I think that we covered a lot today," Michelle said as she brought out her planner again. I nodded my head and pointed to the next date that would work for me. Any of the dates would work for me.

The sooner we do all of this, the sooner my life could go back to being normal.

Chapter Nineteen

"They'll meet you there," I hummed as I got out of the car. I looked back in the car at Luke, Marissa, and Aaron. They were all smushed in Luke's small car but nobody complained about it. Luke took the driver's seat since it was his car. Marissa was in the passenger seat since her round tummy made it hard for her to sit comfortably in the back. I wasn't upset about it though since I had Aaron to keep me company in the back.

Aaron's been a good sport about everything. He's constantly taking me to the therapy sessions when I was too tired to walk. He's also been involved with all of the lawyers and the entire court process. Despite everything that is going on, he still helps to tutor me, works at the gym, kickboxes, and still finds time to hang out with me after school. He's become such a huge staple in my house that my mom, dad, Luke, and Marissa are all familiar with him and find it weird when he isn't over.

Truthfully, I feel as though he just does not want to go home.

Despite how much time we spend together, Aaron won't open up about what is happening with his mom and him. I don't know if they've found a new place or if he's still living with his uncle. While I hoped that the second one wasn't true, I knew that it was possible. If he and his mom were already struggling to keep their place, I knew that it would be difficult for them to keep going without downsizing. He probably doesn't want to distract me during my trial but I was curious about it. I wanted Aaron to know that he was my best friend and that he could trust me with that information if he wanted to. I hoped he still didn't think I was so shallow. He has helped me with so much that I wanted to help him with what he needed. I wanted to prove that I can be his friend too.

As Luke pulled away, I watched his car disappear around the corner. It would only take them about five minutes to get to the courthouse from here. It was in great proximity to each other and from the police station - it was almost right in the middle. Location was probably one of their most important factors.

I bounded down to the basement and slumped into a seat with a thud. I waited about ten seconds before I reached for the phone and held it up to my ear. This was the earliest I have ever been here and it didn't seem like too many people were in the office right now. I felt myself begin to sweat at the thought that something could go wrong.

"Hi, I'm here for Michelle." I paused as the other person on the end scribbled something down. "My name is T-Chloe and today is my court hearing. She said that she would be there so that I am not intimidated by the defendant." I waited a beat before I put the phone back on the receiver.

I breathed out and forced myself to sit back in my chair. My legs were jittering, I was biting my cheeks, and

I kept picking at the skin around my fingernails. I knew that this anxiety I had was not going to go away until I was done with the hearing. Until I was done with everything that has been going on. Until the final verdict was said aloud and I could watch this horrid man go to jail.

I wanted my life back.

Though this entire process has taken longer than I could have imagined, I am glad that I had enough willpower to go through with it. Michelle had really helped me work through my emotions and the events that had happened to me. While still embarrassing to talk about, I was more open to what had happened. Once I was willing to admit that I was a victim, my mental stability had improved. I wasn't lashing out at people. I wasn't boiling over and yelling. I wasn't always angry. I wasn't trying to punish myself with exercise anymore. I was finding better ways to cope.

The hardest thing to admit was that this would affect me for the rest of my life. What had happened to me was not normal – nor was it my fault. The anger and sadness will always be there but it felt better to know that what I was feeling was okay. There may be weeks where I am fine. However, there may be weeks where I have flashbacks and I may be vulnerable.

Michelle wanted me to bring my family once or twice but I still couldn't admit to them that I was coming here. She wanted to encourage them on how to help me if I was having a flashback or a bad week. While it is not an excuse for me not to do things, my mind frame was worse and I may not be as receiving to the male species.

I still found it challenging to not blame all men because of one man.

I still found it challenging to not blame myself.

There were moments that I had with Aaron where I only saw his Uncle. I wasn't able to look at him and while I could see the hurt on his face, I still asked him to leave. Aaron tried to understand but I knew that he didn't. He was hurt by me. I constantly hurt him with my quick changes in behavior.

It's a reason I could never see myself going further with him. There were times in the past couple of months when I thought Aaron would kiss me. There were times in the past couple of months when I thought I was going to kiss Aaron. While it was great at that moment, I knew that I would end up hurting him more. He was helping me in my recovery and he was an amazing friend but I can't like him like that. I wasn't sure if it was a personal wall that I had built up or if it was because I was scared to get attached to anyone - I have yet to talk to Michelle about this yet. She doesn't even know that Aaron exists yet.

I shook my head as I watched someone come in for their day of work. It jostled my mind around and I knew that I would have been stuck in my head for a while if I hadn't noticed her. I looked down at my fingers and saw the little hangnails from the constant picking at my skin and groaned. They would have been healed if I hadn't just picked at them.

"Are you Chloe?" an employee asked. I looked up at her and nodded my head. She smiled at me and held out her hand. I stayed in my seat though and just stared at her hand. Something was off if Michelle wasn't coming to greet me. "I will be escorting you to your court hearing. I'm Dolores." She kept her hand out to greet me but I continued to stare at it. I'm sure my face was running through a mix of emotions.

"Where's Michelle?" I questioned. Her smile faltered and she put her hand near her pants. The smile materialized within a second and as she opened her mouth, I cut her off. "I only trust Michelle."

"Yes, Michelle is an excellent worker." She smiled again but I could see her getting nervous - she wiped her hands on her pants. Her voice was very articulate and she sounded confident. She was good at her job. "However, whoever is on call that day goes with victims to the court." I winced at the word and bit my lip. "That would be me."

"I was told Michelle can come with me." I paused and shook my head. We were not going to get anywhere and I watched as she darted her eyes around the room. "I don't want you with me. I only trust Michelle."

I pushed past Dolores and ventured back up the building. I tried to tell myself to calm down but it was much harder to do when I felt the emotions seeping out of me. The anger was boiling up from the stomach and into my skin - I could feel the heat radiating off of me. When I made it outside, I made sure to stomp so hard on the pavement that it hurt my feet.

What was I supposed to do now? I still had to go to the hearing since my entire family was already there. I still wanted to go but I felt the tears brimming up. When I blinked, they started overflowing and I knew that I had to walk there now. I let myself cry as I thudded against the pavement. I was unprepared for the walking and felt my armpits begin to get moist. I hope it didn't ruin the outfit I was wearing.

"Are you okay?"

I wiped at the tears on my cheeks as Aaron moved me away from my family. I saw Luke look in our direction but he quickly redirected our parents' attention. I nodded my head to thank him and he nodded back as he brought Marissa into the conversation.

"What's up?" Aaron asked. He walked me down the hall so that I could relax on the benches. Nobody could hear me from here. "Where's Michelle?" I shook my head and felt the tears spring into my eyes again. My chin trembled at the threat of me crying and I tried to compose myself. I shook my head repeatedly and Aaron understood that I couldn't talk - my voice would probably crack. "It's okay, you don't need her." He grabbed me by the shoulders and brought me close. I closed the contact between us and felt his hands on my back. "Hey." Aaron let go of me and quietly brought out a little package from his pockets. "You can do this. I have a little present for you." He handed me the present and when I opened the reclosable packing, I stared at it. I had no idea what this was. "It's an anxiety ring," Aaron answered. He shoved it on my finger and started playing with it. "If you get nervous, you can just play with it." I twiddled with it for a second and felt some of the relief coming off of me. "I know you usually play with that necklace from Tanner so I was going to put it on a chain but I didn't want you to-"

"Thank you." I cut him off and smiled at him. He returned the favor and for a second, I felt secure. I grabbed his hand as I heard my name being called down the hall. "I can do this."

"You can do this," Aaron repeated.

***

"How do you think they'll plead?" I questioned my family as I came out of the courtroom. The jury was taking a long time to decide whether or not he was a free man or guilty. My dad was clutching his hands so tightly that his knuckles were turning a ghostly shade of white so I assume he's pretty mad about what happened. Until today, nobody knew in detail what had happened except for the lawyer and Michelle but now they all knew. They all knew how I was dumb to keep going to the after-school sessions and they all probably thought I was a little stupid; I know I did. My mom walked out of the courtroom crying before I even had time to finish my recount. Marissa was there too but she didn't know why until it started. The least to say is she and Luke talked the whole time and she looked like she might cry at any moment. Luke looked like he could hit Craig again—who by the way, had a broken nose. Aaron seemed disgusted by his uncle the entire time and it helped me walk through what happened.

Michelle had prepared me for dealing with the stand. She prepared me for telling everything in front of my family. She let me know that I would be embarrassed. She was right. Anytime an intimate detail was shared, my cheeks blushed red.

"I hope they'll decide that he's guilty," Marissa whispered to me while clutching her round belly. She was due to have the baby at any minute. I wouldn't be surprised if she were to have it within the next week.

"It might be hard though," Aaron told me. "With that false account by my cousin, they might not believe you."

I nodded my head and looked for my mom but she was nowhere in sight. I knew that she might've headed towards the bathroom but I was hoping she would be here for the final decision. I wanted her with me. What was more important than hearing how the person who ruined my life would have the rest of his life determined?

As the doors to the courtroom opened again, I couldn't help but turn around and see him slyly walk with a smirk on his face behind his attorney. I felt my smile fade and my eyes darted towards the ground before I realized that Aaron had also tensed. I placed my arm out in front of him to stop him from whatever he was thinking about doing but all he did was take a good look at me and then his expression softened before nodding his head that he wouldn't do anything he would regret.

Not that he would regret doing it.

"Guys," I whispered. My dad, Luke, Aaron, and Marissa all glanced at me before I looked at Aaron again. "Can I talk to Aaron for a few minutes?" Luke and Marissa nodded their heads and headed out faster than I would've thought possible. When I gave my dad another glance, he nodded his head but he didn't leave. "Alone?"

Finally understanding what I was talking about, my dad scurried out of the hall and I sat on a nearby bench. I waited until Aaron sat down with me before I talked in a hushed tone with him.

"Are you going to have anywhere to stay after?" I asked. Aaron nodded his head no and I placed my hands on top of his. "You could stay at my place."

"Yeah, but my mom, Tanner." I nodded my head for a moment and then sucked my cheeks in. I didn't want to offer Aaron's mom a spot in our house because I was afraid she would have beer all around the house. Or find the beer that is around the house. "Just because one of your problems is being solved, doesn't mean that mine are done being solved."

"I wasn't implying that everything would be normal," I whispered. I shrugged my shoulders and removed my hands from his. "But maybe you should place your mom in a rehab center or something and—"

"Tanner, leave my family alone," Aaron begged. I stared at him for a couple of seconds before I began blinking. How ironic...

"Like you did with mine?" I questioned. Aaron just seemed like he was being slapped in the face. His cheeks sucked in and his jaw tightened before whispering to me—much scarier than yelling at me.

"If it wasn't for me, Tanner, then you wouldn't be getting the justice you deserve." Aaron shot at me. I blinked at him before standing up to his level. I balled my fists up next to my sides and felt my heart breaking with every little stab that Aaron was yelling at me.

"We don't know if he's going to be guilty or not."

"He's guilty, Tanner! He's guilty!" he yelled. He grabbed me by the shoulders and slowly started decreasing his voice. "He's guilty. He's guilty. He's guilty. He's guilty." It got to the point where I thought Aaron was going to break down crying before I did. Instead, we both just sat on the bench again in silence.

"Why are you my friend?" I quietly wondered. "Is it because you feel bad for me? Or is it because you want to make up for what your uncle did to me?" I stared at the ground a little longer and then looked up to see Aaron staring back at me. Once again, he looked shocked like I had slapped him.

"Neither, Tanner." He looked at me and straightened his back while trying to decide which eye to look into for direct eye contact. "Tanner, I'm your friend because I know what it's like to be lonely. Yes, sometimes

I just want to shake you but I know that you want to punch me too." Aaron nodded his head and rolled his eyes before continuing. "And no, I'm not your friend because of what my uncle did to you. That made us closer but I wouldn't stay for that. I stayed because, underneath all of that rock-hard armor of yours, there's a scared little girl. There's a girl who likes to have fun and secretly hates boxing. Underneath your shield, is the girl you used to be. And she just wants to break out," Aaron whispered. I looked at him again before attacking him in a hug. After a few stunned moments, he hugged back.

"You are such a stupid cliché," I whispered. I departed from the hug and just looked at him. Eventually, he started laughing and I couldn't help but laugh along with him. "I appreciate the effort though." My smile slowly faded and I looked at all of the other people in the courthouse.

Everyone had their own stories that I knew nothing about. It was weird to think about. Almost like I didn't know Aaron's story or Luke's story. I'm only a small section of theirs. Like they are only a small section in my story. A girl came out holding her teddy bear while she was crying and whining for her mom while lawyers were talking about her case. A young boy about eleven was going into his courtroom while holding his dad's hand. And the one right across from me was a girl my age and she was hiding her face while trying to hold in tears that were going to escape her tear ducts at any minute.

"Are all of these kids special victims?" I questioned. Aaron looked around and nodded his head. He pointed to the girl with the teddy bear and shuddered. He was here much more often roaming the halls and he's heard about the stories of the others.

"Grandfather." He pointed to the little boy and his face softened. "Dad's girlfriend." He looked towards the teenage girl, who was now crying, and stared at me intensely. "Teacher."

My heart broke, my jaw dropped, my stomach growled, and my eyes watered. I stared with interest at her as her back shook and her hands were up to her eyes so that nobody could see her so childlike. I looked up and down at her and when she picked her head up, I couldn't help but stare as she nodded at the lawyer and then walked herself down the hall and into a courtroom.

"Why didn't she tell?" I whispered in curiosity.

"She did." I looked back at Aaron and he shrugged his shoulders. "Nobody believed her." I wet my lips and felt the pain. The whole time, I kept this secret away from my parents because I didn't think they believed me. If I had just told, then I could've got justice a long time ago. "You're not alone, never."

I looked around the room again and saw a new swarm of people. An old man with his lawyers—already in orange, a beautiful woman with a smirk on her face—in handcuffs, and a tall man being escorted by guards. The defendants. The ones who had hurt these small, powerless children had the nerve to walk through the courtroom like they could walk free at any time.

When Aaron placed a hand on my shoulder, I turned full attention to him and looked at him before hugging him again. I grasped him so hard that I knocked the breath out of him but I didn't care. I continued to squeeze harder and then burst when Aaron squeezed back.

I started crying again.

When I stopped hugging Aaron, I wiped my nose with my sleeve and then my eyes with my fingertips. I looked at him with a whole new perspective and nodded my head multiple times.

"I'm so glad you're my best friend." He nodded his head and then he pressed his back against the bench. I did the same and breathed out. "I guess I should find my mom, she's been gone for a while."

Aaron nodded his head in agreement and I took that as the moment to leave. As I wandered the halls, I was expecting to walk first in on my mom crying in the bathroom but I was a bit baffled when I heard her phone conversation.

As I pressed my ear to the wall, I instantly knew what she was doing. Stomping out of the room, I met Aaron back on the bench—where he didn't move and sat down infuriated.

"Find your mom?"

"Yep."

"Where is she?"

"In the bathroom."

"Is she okay?"

"Just fine."

"What's wrong?"

"Nothing."

"Tanner…" I looked at Aaron and rolled my eyes before giving up and telling him.

"She skipped out in the middle of the court hearing for a job interview on the phone." I crossed my arms and felt defeated. I was just tired of fighting everybody but this was important for me. I wanted my mom to hear it so she knew what I went through. I wanted her to know how much it would've been better if she was a real mom.

If my mom cared she would've stayed during it.

"Maybe she didn't want to hear it." Aaron shrugged his shoulders. "Your dad was crying, Marissa was on the verge of tears, and Luke wouldn't even lookup. The only reason I was staying so strong was that I knew my uncle would love to know what he's done." He shrugged his shoulders when he caught me glancing at him and he patted my back. "Plus, your mom doesn't need to hear all of the gruesome details to know what went on." Aaron shook his head and took a deep breath. "But I think we should go see your father, Luke, and Marissa."

"Why?"

Aaron shrugged his shoulders but he got up anyway. I nodded my head and followed him around the corner to see Marissa sitting with Luke as my dad stared intently at them. As they came to notice me, Marissa thanked me with a kind smile and Luke hurried to include me in the conversation. Dad was making them uncomfortable.

"Did you see mom?" Luke questioned. I nodded my face but Aaron touched him on the shoulder and motioned for him to keep the conversation on that topic on the down-low. "So how are you feeling now that you got that off of your chest?"

"I feel even worse than before I began," I muttered. Aaron looked at me without hesitation but I just stared back without shrugging my shoulders. I was directly implying that to him so he could know how bad I felt. "But I guess you'll all forgive me eventually."

"What?" dad asked. He straightened his back against the bench and looked at me while uncrossing his arms. "You think we're mad at you?" I nodded my head and stared at dad confusingly. "We're not mad at you, Chloe. If anything we're mad at him for not telling us sooner." Dad motioned to Aaron and I looked back to see him shuffling his feet. "Or him for even doing it." Dad looked towards Craig and I couldn't help but stutter as I saw him smile as he was deep in his conversation. "We would never be mad at you for something you didn't have control over." Dad got up from the bench and came over to hug me uncomfortably. "If anything, we're just a tad bit disappointed because you didn't tell us."

There it was. I knew they were something with me; I just wasn't sure what it was. I knew my dad was trying to do a pep talk but right now, that wasn't even helping. I could tell that my dad was a bit uncomfortable, so I smiled and showed him that I was all right. I was used to faking a smile anyway.

"Oh." I heard Marissa say. I looked down at her sitting on the bench and saw her place the palms of her hands on her round belly. I looked at her quizzingly as her face grew more and more serious. "Oh." This time it was a tad bit uncomfortable and Luke grabbed her hands and asked what was wrong. "My water broke."

Chapter Twenty

"Mom's going to kill all of us when she sees that we abandoned her at the court hearing," Luke said nervously. I didn't say anything as I stuck my nose in the air. If she didn't want to be there for me when I needed her the most, it made me feel good that she wasn't here for Luke in his big moment either. It just showed that she valued work more than family. In an instant, my smug look turned into a wince when I heard the screams of Marissa. I wanted to block my ears. She was so loud. I feel like I should not be able to hear her from the waiting room. When I got over the shock, I looked next to me at Luke. The father of this child.

"Shouldn't you be in there?" I questioned. Luke nodded his head and licked his lips. "Why aren't you?"

"What assistance would I be?" he asked. "I can't even look at blood without squealing like a fat pig. I passed out once when you had loose teeth when you were little." I raised my eyebrows but remained quiet as the disturbance of the yelling grew quieter. I hadn't known that about Luke. When I saw a horde of doctors and nurses leaving the room, I knew that the baby was born.

Luke immediately got up and escorted himself to the room. I knew that he wanted to be a supportive father but he already missed the mark by missing his child's birth. Instead, my dad had to be in there with Marissa. I'm sure they would be bickering and arguing about it later. It would be a funny tale to tell one day but even I knew it was a dumb move to make now. When I watched the door to see if anybody would tell me to come in, Aaron scooted closer to me and sat where Luke had been before.

"Do you know if you're going to make it back to hear the final verdict?" Aaron asked. I nodded my head and attempted to chew my nails a bit before I looked over at Aaron. I was nervous as is without him badgering me on getting back in there. I wanted to enjoy the moment where I became an aunt, not wondering if the guy who touched me would be found guilty. I didn't want him to take over my thoughts. I want my good memories to stay good memories. He didn't need to pop in all of them. "Is your mom going to pick you up?"

"Most likely. My dad will probably call her and tell her about the birth of the little baby." I shrugged my shoulders and remained silent with Aaron. We listened for baby cries or Luke's muttering but it was quiet.

Eventually, my dad came out and ushered me inside. He refused to let Aaron in and when I turned around, he also didn't come back in. I was confused when they closed the door behind me but sat beside Marissa as I looked at her. Her hair was gross and she was sweating nervously. I guess giving birth took a lot out of someone. I didn't even want to look at her like that but she already started talking. I had to listen and it would have been rude if I was staring somewhere else while she was talking.

"I obviously won't be there for the rest of the court hearing and I'm sorry that you had to wait so long to get the justice you deserve." She squirmed in her bed so that she could turn and look at me. She smiled a bit and breathed in heavily. "I'm really sorry that you had to sit out on the bench for five hours. I honestly thought that you would've been gone by now." I was slightly offended but didn't say anything as she wiped the sweat off of her forehead. "I mean, I thought court hearings were done in a couple of minutes, at least the ending." She shrugged her shoulders for a minute and I copied her movement. "So do you want to know what we decided to name our girl?" she asked.

I smiled down at her but didn't really care to hear the details of what they named her. I was just ecstatic to know that they had a girl. I mean, I could've dealt with a little boy but I always wanted a sister. This will probably be the closest to a little sister I'll ever get. The only problem with being a girl is when she becomes a teenager. Inside my head, I wondered if she would be one of those types of girls who are popular but snobby or a really nice shy girl. I wondered if she would be smart or athletic. Or both!

As my mind raced with ideas, I didn't register that Marissa's mouth was moving until my mind went blank and my face felt pale. I gulped and looked back down at Marissa to make sure she knew what she was saying. She nodded her head and I felt some sweat appearing on my forehead.

"We named her Leanne." She smiled sweetly at me but at that moment, she seemed nervous around me. She seemed too embarrassed to tell me why she named her daughter after my middle name. At the same time, she kept saying the same things repeatedly. "After you."

"But… why?" I questioned. Marissa pressed her lips together hard and then shook her head slightly. She turned the overhead TV off so that we could be in serious talking mode and she only slightly smiled. I think she was a fed up that I didn't know why at first.

"I want my daughter to be like you." She smiled at me again but rested her head against the pillow and closed her eyes. She sighed deeply and I could guess that she was tired. Within a few minutes, her breathing turned peaceful and a slight snore came out of her mouth.

I looked over at Luke for a second and he nodded his head for me to follow him. When we opened the door, my dad and Aaron were looking at us expectedly. However, Luke ignored both of them and I followed him to the cafeteria. We quickly bought some food and he sat down near an end table. Just like me, he didn't like others hearing our conversation. When I placed my tray on the table, I took quick notice that Luke didn't actually get anything. Was he too nervous to eat? Too excited?

"Why did you name your daughter after me?" I wondered. Luke nodded his head in a weird rhythm but I knew he was just wondering what to say. I took another bite before realizing that the food was garbage and plopped it back on my plate. "I mean, don't you want your daughter to be something else? I'm sorry that Marissa suggested it. I feel like I'm going to be a bother for you forever now."

"Tanner," Luke said, shaking his head at me. He looked at the food with disgust and mutely asked if he could take the tray. I nodded yes but before he left I plopped one last napkin on the tray, the one that I used to wipe the grease off of my chin. When Luke came back, he seemed much calmer and that he knew what he wanted to say and exactly how he wanted to phrase it for me. "I suggested that our baby girl be named after you."

"But..." My eyebrows knitted together in confusion and I felt my jaw open slightly. "Why?"

"Because you're brave." I was still confused but apparently, Luke wasn't done explaining because he continued onwards with what he was saying without actually looking at me. "Sure, if I didn't know what you were going through before our child was born, I would not want her named after you." He shrugged his shoulders and I felt eyes wander to his knee—which was shaking uncontrollably. "And yes, I'm not proud of how you handled the situation—"

"How did I handle the situation?" I questioned harshly. Luke's face instantly went from calm to a face that made it sure that he knew I was just playing dumb. Although I knew what he was talking about in the exact form, I just wanted to hear him say it to me. "Better yet, how would you have handled the situation?"

"I would've told."

"I tried." My voice remained low at his accusation and I shook my head. I knew that he was trying to be helpful but he was rubbing me the wrong way. "If it wasn't for you, I wouldn't be needing to go to court." As soon as I said it, I plopped my hand over my mouth. It was just one of those stupid things you said out of anger to someone. I could see Luke's forehead creased with worry and yelled at myself silently. He blamed himself already, there was no need for me to say that.

"Don't blame this on me, Tanner." His voice was calm as he said it but I knew that he was hurt. He stood up and started walking away from me. As he did this, I apologized profusely but he just kept shaking his head at me. Halfway down the hall, he turned towards me. His face was getting red and blotchy and I knew that he was angry with me now. "At least I wasn't the one that was stupid enough to keep going back!"

I felt like I was slapped across the face. I stared into Luke's eyes for a couple of minutes but it took him too long to realize what he had said was a bad thing to say. I shook my head at him and pouted a bit. He did the same thing to me. He had said something he didn't mean to say out of anger.

"It was a nice offer but I don't want your daughter named after me. Because if your daughter ever went through what I did, you failed as a parent," I whispered so softly.

I walked away while nodding my head but could only escape Luke for a short time. I sat next to Aaron in the waiting room with my dad and when Luke came back, he just acknowledged me a bit before going in with Marissa.

"Mom's going to be here any minute, Tanner," dad said. I nodded my head with a questioned expression but he just shook his head. "Aaron and I are staying here." I turned towards Aaron and he nodded his head in agreement. "Well, you and mom are coming back either way. She wants to see the baby and Aaron doesn't want to take the risk of seeing his uncle again," dad told. I nodded my head in understanding and grabbed my jacket before heading off towards a window where I could see parked cars.

I stared out of it for a while until Aaron decided to show up beside me. I nodded at his presence but he just continued to look out in the view.

"So the baby…" Aaron said. I nodded my head without much to say. Thankfully, I didn't need to talk because Aaron changed the subject entirely. "So are you ever coming back to the gym?"

I thought a bit and breathed out a sigh of relief. "No. Like you said at the courthouse, I really don't like it. I just did it for protection." I continued staring out the window as I saw my mom's car approach. Aaron noticed too so he gave me a quick hug and we stared at each other for a bit before I started leaving.

"Go kill them, Tanner." I looked back at Aaron and gave him a thumbs up. He returned the favor and I looked at him with a sad smile on my face.

"Call me Chloe."

I didn't pause to see his reaction because before I knew it, I was running out to the car my mom was parked in. I barely got buckled in before we took off and my mom sped the whole way back.

"Go, Chloe!"

As my mom parked the car, I ran into the courthouse by myself. I wasn't sure how much time I had left but I knew it wasn't a lot. She promised that she once she found a spot to park, she would be in. I was just hoping I could count on her this time.

The hustle and bustle was odd compared to what it was like before. Lawyers were whispering and running around. Anxiety was probably through the roof of everyone. When I found my lawyer, I stepped beside her and she forced me inside the courtroom. I have been trying to avoid staring at Craig as much as I could. Now that I was seated at the opposite end of the room, I knew it would be easier.

When all was settled, I looked back to see if my mom was sitting in a bench chair but was quite disappointed to see that she wasn't. When my attorney knocked me on my shoulder, I straightened my back and looked at the judge. I needed to pay attention and even if my mom isn't here yet, I knew I could count on her like I could try to count on this system.

"Has the jury finally reached a verdict?"

"We did, your honor."

"How does the jury find the defendant?"

"We find the defendant *not* guilty, your honor."

AMY KULP

National Sexual Assault Hotline
(800) 656 - 4673

ABOUT THE AUTHOR

Amy Kulp is a middle school math teacher with a passion for writing. She had been writing Innocent for almost ten years before deciding she wanted to publish. Wanting to bend the traditional guidelines for the genre, she wanted to write about heavy topics that aren't usually included in the YA section without having a main romance storyline.